# GIANNA POLLERO

# Monster Doughnuts

illustrated by

Sarah Horne

First published in Great Britain in 2021 by
PICCADILLY PRESS
80–81 Wimpole St, London W1G 9RE
www.piccadillypress.co.uk
Owned by Bonnier Books
Sveavägen 56, Stockholm, Sweden

Text copyright © Gianna Pollero, 2021
Illustrations copyright © Sarah Horne, 2021

This is a work of fiction. Names, places, events and incidents are either
the products of the author's imagination or used fictitiously. Any resemblance
to actual persons, living or dead, is purely coincidental.

A CIP catalogue record for this book is available from the British Library.

ISBN: 978-1-84812-943-6

Printe                                                                    A.

*For Sophia and Oscar*

# CHAPTER ONE

# A Monster Bites the Dust

The monster's breath was awful. What was it with monsters and their breath? It was always so bad. She might have only been ten but, coming from a long line of monster-hunters, Grace had smelled her fair share of stinky monster mouths, and this was right up there with the worst.

Grace could see that this particular monster was actually quite small. It sat on the bedroom windowsill holding a flowery curtain over its face, so just its mischievous eyes were showing. She could still see the lower part of its wispy, shadow-like body beneath the pink material.

It constantly changed shape, swirling round and round, up and down.

Grace had no doubt it was a standard Under The Bed Beast – a UTBB for short. She had seen these crafty little creatures a hundred times before. They were one of the most common monsters to bother children and, while they weren't especially dangerous, they caused an awful lot of sleepless nights. Luckily, since they were made – quite literally – out of shadows, they weren't particularly quick or strong, and this made them very easy to destroy.

Grace was standing on an old copper drainpipe, her chest level with the windowsill. She held on tightly with one hand while the other clutched a pot of silvery powder – the best possible mixture for destroying this type of monster. She began to prise the lid off with her thumb but, as she did so, one of her feet slipped and some of the powder fell to the ground.

'Right, shadow boy, you're dust!'

said Grace. She lifted the pot just as her phone rang inside her pocket.

'Really? Now?' she grumbled, reaching inside her school blazer. It was Danni, her older sister.

'Bad time, Dan,' she said.

'Is everything okay? You're a bit late. Are you on your way home?' said Danni.

'I am. Well, I was,' Grace corrected herself. 'But I saw a UTBB in someone's house so I've stopped off to sort it out. Won't take a minute.'

'You're there now? How did you get in?' asked Danni.

'Well, I'm not really *in*,' said Grace, looking at the ground below her.

'Do I even want to know what that means?' asked Danni suspiciously.

'Probably not. But it's not the best time for a phone call,' said Grace. The creature dropped the curtain from its face, ready to swish away from the window.

'No, you don't!' she mumbled to the UTBB. 'Sorry, Dan, gotta go. I'll be home soon. And I've got something interesting to show you!'

She thrust the phone back into her blazer pocket and, with lightning speed, distributed a

cloud of silvery dust from the pot. With a hissy crackle then a putrid *poof*, the monster vanished into thin air.

'Easy peasy,' said Grace to no one in particular, as she started her return journey down the drainpipe.

# CHAPTER TWO

# Monsters LOVE Cakes

Grace flung open the bright yellow door to her family's bakery, Cake Hunters, a good forty-five minutes after she should have been home. The smell of fresh bread, sweet pastries and rich coffee enveloped her, like a big hug, the moment she stepped inside.

Danni had taken charge of the bakery after the sisters' parents had gone missing on a particularly dangerous monster-hunt two years before. Danni was a naturally brilliant pastry chef and she soon had the little bakery bursting at the seams — not only with every cake, biscuit, tart and pie

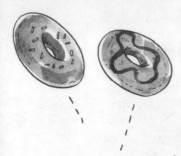

imaginable, but also with customers. There was often a queue of eager croissant-eaters snaking out of the door first thing in the morning.

Luckily, Danni's baking genius also included the ability to make some very special cakes and treats. Ones containing a lot more baking powder than normal cakes. Ones that exploded monsters.

It had been the girls' grandad, Jim Hunter, who had found out about baking powder's monster-destroying properties, quite by accident, when a Pie Pincher made its way into the bakery one day back in the 1950s. With no equipment to hand, he had grabbed the nearest things and chucked them at the monster. One particularly well-aimed throw sent an unsellable scone with too much baking powder in it directly into the monster's mouth – and exploded him on the spot. Jim realised he'd made a ground-breaking discovery.

In the two years since their parents went missing, Grace and Danni had added their own research to their mum's and had built up an impressive list of almost every monster's favourite cake. Danni was kept busy with the bakery, which meant that Grace was left to get on with what she did best. Monster-hunting.

Grace sped past a customer who was closing the lid on an enormous cake box containing a mountainous chocolate cake. A glimpse inside, as she whizzed past, revealed a shiny glaze of icing and shards of dark, milk and white chocolate poking out of the surface of the cake like the tops of icebergs. The sticky sweetness filled Grace's nostrils as she rushed past.

'This is what I need to show you!' she said, waving a colourful piece of paper as she passed Danni, who was standing behind the bakery's counter.

Grace plonked herself into one of the comfy chairs in the seating area at the back of the bakery and put the piece of paper down on the table in front of her.

Within seconds, Danni had joined her. She put a bowl of leftover cookie dough in front of Grace.

'You're right, that is interesting!' said Danni, wiping her hands on her apron and sitting down.

'Jack in Reception drew it,' said Grace. 'Another monster, Danni! There seem to be so many more than usual.'

All the little kids at school came to tell Grace about the monsters that had been bothering them. And she had heard about a lot in the last week or two: Sock Stealers, Homework Takers, Bath Dwellers, Mess Makers . . . There had been so many, Grace was beginning to worry that a gateway to Monster World, where all the monsters came from, had accidentally been left open and unguarded.

'And this is one of the very worst sorts,' said Danni. 'Yikes, it's UGLY!'

The scrawly crayon drawing showed a revolting, fat, mouldy-green monster with one big yellow eye in the middle of its head. A wide grin was spread across its huge face. It was a cyclops. The type of monster that Grace and Danni hated the most.

'Jack said his name is Mr Harris,' said Grace.

Danni frowned. 'Strange name for a monster. Where did he see him?'

'Riding a bike past his house last week, and then again this morning before school,' replied Grace. 'I can't believe there's a cyclops in town. I *HATE* cyclopses.'

'You mean cyclopes,' Danni corrected her.

'Sy-cloh-peez,' Grace repeated, rolling her eyes but smiling. 'Cyclopses or cyclopes, they are all revolting and need exploding. And apparently this one STINKS too.'

'What of?' asked Danni.

'The worst poo you can imagine, and a bit like mouldy cheese,' said Grace, repeating what Jack had told her.

Danni wrinkled her nose. 'Charming. How did Jack know his name?'

She handed a bowl of leftover cookie dough to Grace. 'He heard him say it when he saw him riding the bike. He said he was shouting for people to move because Mr Harris, VIP, was coming through.'

Danni raised her eyebrows. 'Interesting. I'm sure I've read that cyclopes are full of themselves.'

'They'd be full of exploding powder if I got my hands on them,' said Grace, standing up. 'In fact, I'm tracking this one down right now! Don't move, Mr Harris, I'm coming to get you.'

# CHAPTER THREE

# Deadly Doughnuts

She ran up the stairs two at a time and burst into the tiny study at the top of the bakery. The attic room may have been small but it was Grace's monster-hunting headquarters. Endless books and her parents' research journals lined the walls and balanced precariously on the mantelpiece of the old iron fireplace. For generations, hunting monsters had been her family's purpose. Skills, equipment and knowledge had been handed down for hundreds of years. Above the fire hung a collection of family portraits, with a painting of her grandad, Jim, in the middle. He had been photographed holding a glass jar with a very grumpy-looking leprechaun inside. Jim had a net over one shoulder and a wide grin on his face. The leprechaun wore a green hat and was picking its nose.

Grace strode straight over to the computer in the middle of the cramped room and hit the 'on' button.

'Right then, Mr Harris, let's find out a bit more about you,' Grace said as she pulled Jack's drawing from her pocket. She typed in his name then fed the sketch into a slot on the machine. Within seconds, a 3D version of Jack's picture came up on the screen, bringing Mr Harris very much to life. The cyclops's outline revolved slowly, showing off all his disgusting features.

'Holy moly,' said Grace. She hadn't realised from Jack's drawing how big this one-eyed monster actually was. The information claimed he was 2 metres tall and weighed 275 pounds.

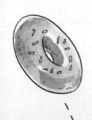

14

'That's more than a baby elephant,' Grace whispered.

Although this particular cyclops was rather flabby, Grace could still see the shape of powerful muscles under his droopy, green-tinged skin. His gullet was enormous, a bit like a frog's, which made him even more repulsive. The bones of his spine ran in a line down the middle of his wide back, and some tufts of wiry black hair sprouted from beneath his shoulders.

Grace scanned the information on the Monster Scanner.

## MONSTER

**Name**: Mr Harris

**Type**: Cyclops

**Age**: Approximately 352

**Height**: 2 metres

**Weight**: 275 lbs

**Strengths**: 12 detected: power, sense of smell,

body mass, confidence, keeping promises, Snakes and Ladders, fighting skills, eyesight, ability to hypnotise, memory, Frisbee and chess.

**Weaknesses**: 1 detected: iced doughnuts

**Likes**: Iced doughnuts, being important, politics, eating people who annoy him, board games, jokes, riding bicycles, *Britain's Got Talent*.

**Dislikes**: Rude humans, too many humans, avocados, his grandfather, Neville Harris.

**Best form of destruction**: Iced doughnuts, baking powder, sharp object to centre of eye.

**Notes**: Has a tendency to eat people with little or no warning.

## SCORING:

**Friendship**: 0

**Size**: 87

**Courage**: 74

**Kindness**: 0

**Intelligence:** 71 (please note, this is above average for this breed of monster)

**Loyalty:** 0

**Violence:** 99

**Danger:** 100

**Type:** Rare (mainly due to unusual intelligence for a cyclops)

'Brilliant,' said Grace sarcastically. 'If you were a Top Trump, Mr Harris, I'd be playing your danger skills.'

She read further down the page. What she really wanted to know was where to find the revolting creature. Next to the word 'Location' on the screen was an egg timer. The Monster Scanner was having to work hard to find Mr Harris's whereabouts.

'Come on,' whispered Grace. It never usually took more than three or four seconds.

Just as she was about

to go and get a cup of tea, the Monster Scanner beeped loudly and the egg timer disappeared.

Location: Houses of Parliament, London

'That can't be good . . .' Grace's breath caught in her throat as she pressed the 'print' button. She had to go and find Mr Harris!

# CHAPTER FOUR

# The Appointment

Mr Harris chained his bicycle a short distance from the Houses of Parliament, pulled his sleeves down and adjusted his glasses.

'Clever glasses!' He chuckled.

The glasses were large and black-rimmed, and had eyes painted over the lenses. They looked so realistic that only someone who stared at them for a good minute might work out that they were fake. And by that time, chances were that person would have been hypnotised by Mr Harris's real eye, which lurked behind the glasses, smack bang in the middle of his forehead.

He hummed as he walked towards the visitors' entrance of the magnificent building.

'Identification, please, sir,' said the security officer guarding the door.

'Ah yes, identification,' repeated Mr Harris, patting down his jacket. He found what he was looking for and flashed a card at the security officer.

'Sorry, sir, that's a library card. I hate to say it, but you don't look much like a Doris Jones,' said the officer, raising his eyebrows. 'Do you have some actual identification with you? I can't let you in without it.'

As the security officer reached for his walkie-talkie, Mr Harris lowered his glasses just a few millimetres and allowed his big yellow eye to reveal itself.

'Urgh, wuh, aargh!' yelped the security officer.

Hastily, Mr Harris pushed his glasses back up his nose. 'Hush hush,' he soothed. 'You mustn't be a pest. Mustn't get in the way.

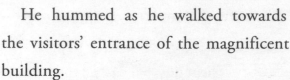

I'm very important. I'm on my way to see the Prime Minister.'

The security officer nodded like a zombie. 'Yes, sir, of course, sir. Please come in, you mustn't be late for your appointment.'

'Thanks, Rufus!' said Mr Harris, reading his name badge and patting his new favourite security officer so hard on the back that he fell over.

'Whoopsie!' said Mr Harris with a giggle.

He stepped over Rufus and wandered in.

## CHAPTER FIVE

# Monster-Ready!

'How many do you think you'll need?' asked Danni, holding up two doughnuts in each hand.

'Just give me all of them. He's enormous,' Grace replied, wrenching her rucksack open.

Danni picked up a silver tray of doughnuts from behind the counter and tipped them all into Grace's bag. There were at least a dozen.

Grace hastily scanned the rest of her equipment, some of which was hidden in the secret compartment of her rucksack, ticking things off in her head.

- Sketch book and pencil.

- Large pot of baking powder.

- Camera.

- Bag containing a selection of baked goods generally liked by monsters – ginger nuts, choc-chip cookies, half a blueberry muffin, a sourdough roll, jam tarts, most of a macaroon.

- Catapult.

'Be careful, Grace,' said Danni. 'This is a cyclops. We don't have a good track record with those dudes.'

'I know, and I will be,' said Grace, allowing herself to think fleetingly about her parents, who had disappeared while hunting down a cyclops.

'Are you really going right now?' asked Danni.

'Got to,' said Grace, swinging the bag onto her back. 'He must be at the Houses of Parliament for a reason. And it can't be a good one, so I need to act fast. Hopefully, if it all goes to plan, that freaky cyclops will be dust before tea-time.'

Danni nodded, but she didn't look happy.

'I could close the bakery a couple of hours early, then I could come with you. Have you got enough baking powder?' she fussed, shoving another tub into Grace's hand instead of waiting for an answer.

'No,' Grace said firmly. 'Mum and Dad made the mistake of going on a hunt together, and look what happened. Anyway, you know there's nothing I'm better at than wiping out monsters single-handedly. I'm up to forty-seven this month already, if you count the UTBB from earlier. It's my personal best!'

'I know, and it's only the fifteenth of July,' said Danni, shaking her head in disbelief.

Grace laughed. 'Wish me luck!'

'Good luck. Be safe, sis,' said Danni.

'I'll be fine,' Grace reassured her. 'I just can't say the same for Mr Harris!'

CHAPTER SIX

# A Doughnutty Distraction

Twenty minutes later, Grace found herself racing down a plush corridor in the Houses of Parliament, looking for a cyclops. She had got in reasonably easily, by saying she was late for a school trip, and had only had one slightly tricky moment when a suspicious-looking security guard had questioned the number of doughnuts in her bag. Telling him she was constantly hungry, and stuffing a whole one into her mouth, seemed to have convinced him she was genuine.

Grace spotted Mr Harris the moment she entered the Jubilee Café near the entrance to

Westminster Hall. She sneaked her camera out of her rucksack and, quick as a flash, snapped a photo. He was much taller than everyone else there, and a lot wider too. She noticed he had done a pretty good job of covering up as much skin as possible, but the bits she could see – on the lower part of his face and his hands – had a peculiar green tint.

He wore glasses, a hat and a heavy tweed jacket, which looked rather odd when everyone else was dressed for an English summer in light cardigans and linen jackets. But more than anything, what gave him away to Grace was his smell. Jack had been right: he smelled distinctly of really bad poo and mouldy cheese. Grace noticed quite a few people wafting their hands under their noses and looking round to see where the grim stench might be coming from.

Mr Harris seemed unaware of his own off-putting odour. He was wandering along the queue of people waiting to order coffees and cakes. He stopped at each person and asked, 'Excuse me, have you seen the Prime Minister?'

Grace noticed he was surprisingly well-spoken for a cyclops. The ones she had encountered before had barely been able to string a sentence together.

She watched as he became distracted by the cakes behind the counter. He pushed into the queue.

'Excuse me!' said an angry-looking woman behind him. 'Go to the back of the queue! You can't just push in.'

'I'm hungry,' said Mr Harris, not bothering to look at the woman.

'We all are! That's why we are in the queue! Now go to the back!'

'No, thank you,' he replied.

The woman waved her arms to get the attention of a member of staff. She called out, 'This man has pushed in. Could someone please tell him to go to the back of the queue?'

Grace's heart beat faster as Mr Harris looked at the woman.

'You're very annoying,' he muttered.

Grace watched as he fumbled with his glasses. Immediately, the woman stopped shouting.

'Sorry,' she said robotically, her legs began to give way. 'Please do go in front of me.'

Suddenly Grace remembered one of his strengths from the Monster Scanner – the ability to hypnotise! She needed to get him away from the crowd. She ran up behind him.

'Excuse me, sir, did you say you were looking for the Prime Minister?' she said quietly.

He turned slowly. 'Yes, as a matter of fact, I did.'

Grace was careful not to look at his glasses, or what lurked behind them, and instead focused on a scaly patch of greenish skin at the bottom of his chin.

'Well, I know where she is. I can show you if you want.'

Mr Harris looked torn. 'But I'm hungry. Show me in five minutes.'

'She'll have gone by then. You could have one of my snacks while we walk to her office,' Grace said, opening the top of her bag to show him the contents.

Without looking, she knew his eye had opened wide at the sight of the iced doughnuts.

'Yum!' he cried. 'Come on

then, little girl, let's go and eat the Prime Minister! I mean, *meet* the Prime Minister!' He chuckled, putting his enormous hand up to cover his mouth.

Grace's heart was beating fast. *Eat the Prime Minister.* Was that why he was here?

There was no time to lose.

# CHAPTER SEVEN

# Bang!

'This way,' said Grace, leading Mr Harris out of the café and down a long corridor. She planned to get him as far away as she could from the busy areas. No one needed to see a monster explode in front of them at five o'clock on a Friday afternoon. It was often a very messy business and Grace had a feeling the smell Mr Harris would leave behind could have knocked out a rhino.

'Doughnut!' called Mr Harris behind her. She saw him holding out his huge hand.

'Hang on a minute,' she said. 'Let's just get round this corner. I don't want you to miss the

Prime Minister.'

Mr Harris snorted
in disgust and stomped
after Grace. They went past
endless closed doors, glass display
cabinets and winding staircases. The
corridor seemed to go on forever.

'Stop!' bellowed Mr Harris.

Although Grace should have been nervous, she
wasn't. In fact, she felt exhilarated and confident.
She was a monster-hunter, after all. She turned
calmly to the cyclops and said, 'What's the matter?'

'I want a doughnut! You said I could have a
doughnut!' Mr Harris folded his arms across his
chest like a spoiled child.

'For goodness' sake,' said Grace, rolling her
eyes. 'I thought you wanted to see Prime Minister
Attwood? Fine, have a doughnut, but you might
miss her.'

'But I want both!' cried Mr Harris.

'Well, you can't have both.'

'You're mean!' huffed Mr Harris. 'Give me my doughnut.'

'It's not your doughnut, it's my doughnut,' said Grace. 'Now, say please.'

Mr Harris scowled.

'Say it!' said Grace. 'You'll never get to see the Prime Minister if you can't even say please.'

'Please,' Mr Harris mumbled, super-quietly, his head cast down towards the floor.

Grace looked down the corridor. There didn't seem to be anyone around. She took a deep breath and opened her bag. Mr Harris shuffled forward, peering inside the rucksack.

'You've got lots!' he cried. 'Yummy!' His hand darted out and grabbed a doughnut. He swallowed it whole. 'Another one!' he shouted.

'Another one, what?' said Grace, wondering how many it would take to explode the one-eyed beast. She hoped she had brought enough.

'PLLEEEEASE!' shrieked Mr Harris, jumping up and down. An ornate china vase in a glass cabinet wobbled from side to side.

'Shhhh!' said Grace, looking round. 'Noisy people get thrown out of places like this.' She handed him another two doughnuts.

He threw them up into the air and they spiralled downwards into his mouth.

'More!' he demanded.

Grace tossed two more over to him. This time, rather than eating them in one bite, he took a mouthful out of one and popped the other one onto a finger on his left hand, like a ring.

'Do you work here?' Mr Harris asked, licking the icing.

'Yes,' said Grace with no hesitation.

'You seem too young and small to work here,' he replied. 'What's your job?'

'I bring the doughnuts to sell in the cafés.'

'Doughnut Lady!' giggled Mr Harris.

'What's your name?' ventured Grace.

Mr Harris puffed his chest out, which made him look even bigger, then, as though he was announcing a royal visitor, he said, 'I am Mr Harris.' Then added, 'And you can call me . . . Mr Harris.'

'Okay, Mr Harris. So why are *you* here?' asked Grace, willing the baking powder to do its job.

'I've said already, to eat the Prime Minister,' said Mr Harris, popping the last piece of the first doughnut into his mouth. 'I mean, *meet* the Prime Minister.' He sniggered behind his doughnut jewellery.

Grace shuddered. 'I see. Why do you want to *meet* her?'

'Too many questions, Doughnut Lady!' said

Mr Harris, shovelling the treat on his finger into his mouth. 'You look like someone I know,' he said. 'She asked a lot of questions too.'

Grace's heart skipped a beat. 'Who?'

'She was annoying! And so was the man she was with. And they were trying to get rid of me! SO rude,' said Mr Harris, tutting. 'Anyway, they've gone, so never mind.'

Grace's skin tingled. 'What do you mean?'

Mr Harris stopped chewing.

'TOO MANY QUESTIONS!' he bellowed, straightening up to his full height. He moved his hand up towards his glasses.

Grace reached into her bag for the tub of baking powder Danni had given her. She was *not* going to let him hypnotise her.

As she drew her arm back, ready to throw the tub, Mr Harris stopped dead in his tracks.

'My tummy feels funny,' he said frowning.

And then he exploded.

# CHAPTER EIGHT

# Never Upset a Werewolf

Bright lights of every colour imaginable spiralled round Mr Harris's head as he spun away, completely out of control. This happened every time he exploded. He travelled at an alarming speed and usually ended up crash-landing, on his bottom, somewhere highly inconvenient. Most monsters that exploded, just exploded. Some made an absolute mess, with guts and slime everywhere, while others just poofed into a pretty, glittery cloud. And then they were gone. Permanently. But not Mr Harris. He rocketed straight back to the place he had come from: the one place he didn't want to be. Monster World.

And here he was again.

'My bottom!' he moaned. 'I blame Doughnut Lady!'

Suddenly, there was a deafening howl behind him. Mr Harris whipped round. A crowd of about fifty monsters of all shapes and sizes glared at him. A tiny werewolf wearing a purple party hat stood at the front, his hairy head thrown back as he howled and sobbed.

Mr Harris looked down. He was sitting in the middle of a very large birthday cake. He could just make out some words in icing: **Happy 3rd birthday Gil–**. The rest was a gloopy mess.

'Whoops!' said Mr Harris cheerfully. 'Who left that there? Never mind, no harm done. And happy birthday, Gil!' He slid off the table on a sheet of fondant icing.

'My name . . . is . . . Gilbert!' cried the tiny werewolf.

'Urgh, why? That's a terrible name for a werewolf,' said Mr Harris.

'IT'S A FAMILY NAME!' thundered a voice from the crowd. A huge werewolf pushed through and scooped up Gilbert, who was crying so loudly that some less polite monsters had covered their ears – or were trying to poke napkins and balloons into them – to drown out the noise.

Mr Harris stood up briskly, scooping an enormous piece of the squashed cake into one hand, which he held behind his back.

'Oh, a family name? Very good. Very strong.' Mr Harris gave the monsters a thumbs-up with the hand that wasn't covered in cake. 'Right, I must be off.'

With that, he ran as fast as a 275-lbs cyclops could through the crowd of monsters to find his way back to London, only stopping to pick up a chunk of Victoria sponge that fell out of his hand on the way.

# CHAPTER NINE

# Prodding a Monster

'It took five doughnuts!' Grace said to Danni as they ate supper: tomato soup with fresh bread from the bakery. 'It's so annoying that he blew up just as he was saying something interesting, but I'm sure he was going to try and hypnotise me.'

Danni raised one eyebrow. 'It's a good job he did blow up, then.'

'Meh. I could've held him off for a bit longer,' said Grace, dunking bread into her bowl. 'He told me I looked like someone he knew. A woman he had got rid of, along with a man. What if he was talking about Mum and Dad? I look like Mum – everyone says so.'

Danni sighed. 'It's possible, I suppose. But we both know how dangerous monsters can be. The chances of them being alive are . . . well, not great.'

'We can't give up, Dan,' said Grace. 'I still miss them so much, and I'm sure they're still out there somewhere. We've never had any actual proof that they're dead, have we? We can't let the monsters win this one.'

Danni nodded and ruffled her sister's dark hair, smiling at the look of determination on Grace's face. 'I know, and you're right. I miss them too and we must never give up hope. I just don't want you to get killed because you're prodding a monster for information when, really, you should just be blowing it up.'

'Who doesn't love prodding a monster?' Grace said cheerily. 'Especially when you can explode them spectacularly too. I've never seen anything like today! There were lights and sparks and a sort of rumbling, whooshing noise. It was quite amazing. The smell was BAD though.'

'Gross,' said Danni. 'I'm glad you do the hands-on stuff. Do you remember that vicious Sock Stealer that smelled of raw onions? Urgh!

GIVE ME SOCKS!

What was its name again?'

Grace nodded and pulled a face. 'Niffy McWhiffy. Won't ever forget him, stinky little beast! But you'd have hated this cyclops explosion. It reeked. Like a mixture of rotten eggs, off milk, mouldy cheese and icing sugar. Grim. Anyway, I'm going to go and put him in the "Dead" folder on the Monster Scanner.'

Grace raced up the stairs, two at a time.

She flicked the switch to the Monster Scanner and dropped into her dad's leather chair. The smell of the chair reminded her of him so much. Fleetingly she allowed herself to remember the way his gangly arms had drooped over the scuffed arm-rests, and the way her mum would cover his legs with a blanket when he'd dozed off in the middle of researching Slime Imps. She blinked away the tears that threatened to spill down her cheeks and tapped determinedly at the keyboard.

A database appeared on the

screen in front of her. She typed Mr Harris – cyclops into the search field and connected her camera to the computer to download the photo she had taken. All she had left to do was mark him as dead and write some notes. Then the details would be stored in the archive of monsters that had been successfully destroyed. Job done!

His profile flashed onto the screen.

**Name**: Mr Harris

**Monster**: Cyclops

**Age**: Approximately 352

**Height**: 2.05 metres (+0.05m since last search)

**Weight**: 285 lbs (+10 lbs since last search)

**Strengths**: 13 detected (+1 since last search): *click here to view*

*Weaknesses, 1 detected: click here to view*

*Likes: click here to view*

*Dislikes: click here to view*

*Best forms of destruction: click here to view*

*Notes: click here to view*

*Scoring: click here to view*

Help

Grace frowned.

'Why is it not giving me the 'dead' option?' she muttered.

She clicked the 'help' button.

**Location**: Unknown

**Alert status**: Critical

'What?' said Grace. 'He exploded. This is impossible!'

She clicked on the detected strengths. How could a dead cyclops have gained another power?

**Strengths**: 13 detected: power, sense of smell, body mass, confidence, keeping promises, Snakes and Ladders, fighting skills, eyesight, ability to hypnotise, memory, Frisbee, chess, improved regeneration time (new).

'Improved regeneration time?' Grace whispered. 'He can regenerate. He's not dead.'

She took in the other information on the screen.

'And somehow he's bigger.'

She flew out of the room and hurtled down the stairs.

'Danni! We've got a problem! An even bigger problem!'

# CHAPTER TEN

# Max Who?

Grace hadn't heard of a monster that was able to regenerate before. An exploded monster usually meant a dead monster, which was exactly how she liked them.

After Grace's surprising discovery about Mr Harris, Danni had rushed to the study to help look through their mum's old journals for any information they could find about cyclopes.

'Have you found much?' Grace asked.

Louisa Hunter had made endless notes about every monster she had seen, heard of and been told about – something her daughters were extremely grateful for as they continued her work.

'Yes!' replied Danni, studying a sketch of a one-eyed monster. 'There's loads of information about cyclopes as a category of monster – self-important, smug, strong, unpredictable, evolving quickly, fond of leisure activities, blah, blah, blah, but look at this, Grace. Look! They knew about Mr Harris!'

Grace leaned over her sister's shoulder and scanned the journal. Her mum's neat handwriting jumped from the pages, full of life, and Grace could almost hear her excitedly reading the words aloud.

Mr Harris (full name unknown): cyclops – oddly intelligent. Likes to disguise himself as human – wears a tweed jacket with leather elbow patches, hat and fake glasses. Interested in politics. Massively sweet tooth.

Grandson of Neville A.Q.T.A.C. Harris – DANGEROUS. Shape-shifter.

These two cyclopes hate each other. If they ever meet again, it could be catastrophic. (Ask Max for more info. Use Monster Scanner – encrypted mode.)

'Max?' said Danni. 'Who's Max?'

'I'm not sure. I didn't know the Monster Scanner could send messages,' said Grace. She grabbed the mouse and began to click through all the familiar menus and screens. There was no option to send anyone a message. As a last resort, she typed 'Max' into the monster search field.

A pop-up screen appeared almost immediately.

Max Hunter – presumed dead.

'Oh! How annoying. Look – he's got the same surname as us!' said Grace.

'That *is* interesting,' Danni replied. 'I wonder who he was. Maybe there's more in Mum's notes? You could keep looking while I go back downstairs. I need to make a sticky toffee pudding and a Bundt cake ASAP.'

'I know sticky toffee puddings are Parent Punishers' favourites, but who likes Bundt cake?' asked Grace, raising her eyebrows. 'And what is Bundt cake?'

Danni laughed. 'It's just a ring-shaped cake. Poo Shufflers LOVE them. And with the number of those that have been reported lately, I'll probably be baking Bundt cakes for the next thirty years.'

Grace nodded. 'There have been a lot, haven't there? Actually, there's been a lot of everything in the last couple of weeks. Sightings are up 74 per cent! I wonder why Poo Shufflers like Bundt cake?'

Danni rolled her eyes. 'Probably because they can sit in the middle of the cake while they scoff it. Disgusting.'

Grace giggled and reached over to the cluttered mantelpiece for more of her mum's notebooks.

'Grace, look – what's that?' said Danni, pointing at the Monster Scanner.

Grace looked at the screen. An alert had popped up in the bottom right-hand corner of the screen.

1 new message.

Grace leapt over and clicked on it.

Louisa? Eamon? Are you back?! M.

'Max?' she whispered.

## CHAPTER ELEVEN

# Frankenstein and the Monsters

'I can't believe we've found another Hunter,' said Grace, unwrapping a jam tart as they sat on an almost empty train to Henley-on-Thames on their way to meet Max in person. 'We never even knew Dad had any cousins.'

'I know,' said Danni, 'and after all this time. I wonder how much he knows. Oh, Grace, watch out!'

Grace had barely any time to look where her sister was pointing before a scruffy-haired, rodent-like monster had hoiked itself onto her lap and snatched her jam tart.

'A Snack Snaffler!' Grace exclaimed, grabbing it by one of its flappy ears. 'On a train? What's going on? There are monsters everywhere!'

The Snack Snaffler dangled from her fingers, kicking its legs and hissing, clinging to the jam tart with its oddly large, furry hands. As she tried to

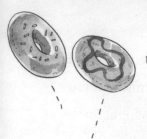

take back her snack, the ratty-looking creature stuffed the whole thing into its mouth and laughed throatily, spraying her with spit and crumbs.

'Do you need the baking powder?' asked Danni, starting to unzip her bag.

Grace shook her head and opened the train window. 'No, I don't usually bother exploding Snack Snafflers. They're quite useful at cleaning up in cinemas and school lunch halls and stuff.'

She flung the creature out of the window and sat back down, reaching into her rucksack for her notebook to record the sighting.

It was a short walk from the station to the House by the River, which stood on its own, surrounded by tall trees and an old brick wall. The house was a vast, beautiful Victorian building with a long winding path that led, through wild flowers, all the way down to an arched front door.

Grace rapped the door knocker – a rather ugly brass gargoyle – full of excitement about meeting Max. Another Hunter.

Almost immediately, the door opened a crack. Then, it stopped.

'Hello?' she ventured. 'Max? It's Grace. And Danni . . .'

The door creaked open a millimetre more, then one more, then one more. When the gap made it to a few centimetres, four shiny metal prongs suddenly appeared and poked their way through into the space.

Grace exchanged a look with Danni. She was about to gently push the door when she heard footsteps thudding towards it.

'Open the door, Frank, there's a good lad,' said a deep but kind voice. 'Nothing to be worried about – it's your cousins. Come on, open it up! Careful you don't prod your fork at them.'

The door opened properly to reveal a smiley, tall, stocky man and a very small, startled-looking boy who held an ornate golden fork in his right hand.

'Grace! Danni! Come in, please,' said the man, beaming at them. 'It's wonderful to see you. I'm Max. And this is Frank. Say hello, Frank.'

'H-hello,' Frank said, lowering his fork.

The girls followed Max and Frank through the spacious entrance hall. Grace noticed that Max walked with a slight limp, and that his left arm was missing. What she could see of his right arm was badly scarred.

Frank skipped along beside Max. Sometimes, he took tiny, cautious steps and at other times, he leapt forward. Every couple of steps, he checked over his shoulder, as though he was expecting something to pounce on him. His head seemed too big for his bird-like body, he had a mass of scruffy blond hair, and the freckles across his nose stood out against his pale skin. He held his ornate gold fork out in front of him, and his black T-shirt was rolled up at the cuffs, clearly too big for his small frame.

Max stopped by a heavy panelled door and said to Frank, 'Go and get your drawing stuff and then we'll all go to the office, okay?'

Frank nodded and scurried through the door.

Max turned to the sisters and said very quietly,

'Frank is a rather nervous child. I rescued him five years ago when I was chasing a particularly troublesome Shadow Stalker and stumbled through a hidden Monster World gateway which, incidentally, we were never able to find again. He was being raised by a family of goblins – who knows where they got him from – with werewolves as neighbours on one side, and a Snot-nosed Ogre on the other. His goblins kept Wardrobe Lurkers as pets, so he was quite literally surrounded by monsters for the first three years of his life. It's no wonder he has a few anxiety issues.'

'Frank is eight?' Danni whispered.

Max nodded. 'He's very small for his age. I'm hoping he will have a growth spurt in the next year or two – that should help his confidence. And, let's be honest, you need something about you when you have a name like Frankenstein.'

'Frank is short for Frankenstein?' Grace muttered.

Max nodded again. 'Goblins. Not my first choice but he was used to it by the time I adopted him.'

'What's the fork for?' asked Danni.

'Self-defence. Goes everywhere with him. I believe it was a christening present from a troll – they love cutlery,' said Max.

Frank reappeared in the doorway with a bundle of papers and sketch books, a variety of coloured pencils balanced on the top. He was still clutching the fork, prongs protruding, in one hand.

'Ready, D-Dad,' he said, giving a nod.

'Excellent!' said Max cheerily. 'Shall we show the girls where we get our work done?'

## CHAPTER TWELVE

# Neville Who?

Grace was not expecting Max to open the office door, which was at the bottom of the rickety cellar stairs, by placing his thumb on a pad which scanned his fingerprint.

She was also not expecting the heavy steel door to open into a huge space containing two sleek desks and leather chairs, glittering screens, paper-thin laptops, digital whiteboards and extensive displays of monster photographs and information, some with strings linking them.

'Whoa! This place is amazing,' she gasped, looking around, struggling to take everything in.

Frank put his papers and pencils on one of the gleaming desks and sat down in a big leather chair. It made him look tiny. He seemed to have relaxed a little and, as he rested his fork on his lap, he said quickly, 'This r-room is 520 metres squared. It contains over 130 pieces of monster-hunting equipment and approximately 10,347 up-to-date m-monster records.'

'Spot on, buddy! Our monster-hunting headquarters,' Max said proudly, leaning against the other gleaming desk. 'Girls, you should know that I work for the Secret Service, so anything we say within these four walls must not be repeated, apart from to each other.'

Grace and Danni nodded.

Max continued. 'When this happened,' he gestured to his missing arm, 'I was working on a major operation to track down a particularly dangerous monster. While I recovered, my boss – Prime Minister Attwood – decided it would be better for everyone to think I was dead, so I could carry on my undercover work completely in secret, once I was better. I have been 'presumed dead' ever since. My neighbours call me Clive Hudson. Of course, your parents knew the truth. When I received your message, I thought it was one of them. I thought they were back. I'm so sorry they're not.' Sadness fell across Max's face.

Danni held out an envelope full of papers from the Monster Scanner along with Grace's notes, the photo she had taken of Mr Harris, and photocopies of information they had found in the journals. 'We brought these,' she said. 'And these.' She held out a box from the bakery.

Max's expression changed immediately. 'You darling girls!' he exclaimed. Within seconds, he had taken an enormous bite out of a gooey custard slice. He held the box towards Frank, who stabbed a chocolate éclair with his fork.

'Good grief, I think these are even better

than when your mum did the baking!' Max said happily. He ate the whole slice before he took the papers and spread them across the desk. He studied them intently while Grace explained everything that had happened in the past twenty-four hours.

When she stopped to catch her breath, Max gathered the papers together and placed them in a pile, then looked at the girls.

'All of this is both fascinating and concerning,' he said. 'The fact you encountered Mr Harris at the Houses of Parliament worries me. It does, however, confirm my suspicions that Mr Harris's grandfather is also in the area. And if that *is* the case, it could be catastrophic. These two cyclopes are in fierce competition, and they hate each other with a passion. I can't tell you strongly enough how dangerous they are – particularly old Gramps, Neville Adolphus Quentin Timothy Artemis Clarence Harris.'

'Neville *who* Harris?' said Grace, stifling a giggle.

Max grinned. 'Ah, yes. Cyclopes, and actually a lot of monsters, have a tendency to make some, let's say, unusual choices when choosing names for their offspring. Take my Frankenstein, for instance . . .'

Frank gave a nervous smile. 'Dad's right. My middle name is just as bad. It's Gruffalo.'

The girls giggled.

'So, Max, why do the two of them hate each other so much?' asked Danni.

'Well,' said Max, leaning forward, 'it's rather complicated. Are you ready?'

CHAPTER THIRTEEN

# Oh My Goblins!

Max took a deep breath. 'The family history is very complex but, really, it's to do with Mr Harris's mother, Gertrudetta, who of course is Neville's daughter. Neville adored Gertrudetta and got very jealous when Mr Harris was born, as he took up all of Gertrudetta's attentions. Then, as Mr Harris grew up, he became envious of Neville's closeness to his mother. He felt that she loved Neville more than she loved him.'

'I get the jealousy thing,' said Danni. 'But it doesn't seem enough for them to really, really detest each other.'

'Ah, well, it doesn't stop there,' said Max. 'There's also what happened at the Monster World Board Game Championships. Monsters love board games almost as much as they love cakes, and they all have their areas of expertise. Frank, which year was the incident?'

hee hee

Frank jumped in. 'It was 1962. Mr Harris took the crown from Neville after the championship final game of Connect 4. The game lasted thirty-one minutes, 7,418 monsters were watching, and one goblin, four Sock Stealers and a bat died.'

'That's right,' said Max. 'So, bearing in mind the hatred was strong before, after that, it was off the scale. That crown is a big deal in Monster World. It's also worth pointing out that one of our relations, Walter Hunter, exploded Neville's wife, Anastasia Clarissa Penelope Adeline Rose Harris, years and years ago. Neville has never forgiven that. It's safe to say that the Hunter family is not at the top of his Christmas card list.'

Grace raised her eyebrows. 'Oh, right. Oops. So they're rivals in every sense. Why did Mr Harris being at the Houses of Parliament make you think Neville is nearby too?'

'We have a photo!' said Frank excitedly, leaning forward in his oversized chair. 'We thought it was him but we weren't completely sure.' Frank pointed to a blurry photo pinned to a noticeboard. It showed a muscular figure with dark hair and slightly green skin. Although its features were unclear, it was plain that only one eye sat in the middle of its forehead.

'Oh!' exclaimed Grace. 'Who took the photo?'

'It was taken by the Monster Radar,' said Max, gesturing to what looked like a satellite dish in the corner of the room. It appeared to be wired up to a printer.

'We programme it to watch certain locations,' said Frank, 'if we think there are monsters there.'

'That photo was taken in London,' said Max. 'In Westminster. So I'm sure now that it's Neville.'

'Sixteen metres from the main entrance to the Houses of Parliament,' added Frank. 'On Friday.'

'The day I exploded Mr Harris!' said Grace.

Max nodded. 'Bingo. Both these cyclopes are power-crazy. For years and years, Neville has gained power in Monster World – and not just because he was reigning champion of the MWBG Championships for over a hundred years. Over time, he's gained the trust and support of hundreds of monsters by showing his strength and ruthlessness and, now . . . I believe he's ready to gain power here. In *our* world. Have you noticed the sudden increase in monster numbers?'

'Yes!' cried the sisters.

'The Monster Radar has picked up 892 sightings this month,' said Frank, gripping his fork more tightly.

Max looked serious. 'We have a situation for sure. I have no doubt that if Mr Harris is trying to get to the Prime Minister, then Neville is too. And I can't stress enough how dangerous he is. I mean, he ate his own mother, if that gives you an idea. The only case of cyclops cannibalism I have ever heard of. And she was a vegan, which somehow makes it worse…'

'Oh my goblins! I didn't know that! D-Dad, what do we need to do?' asked Frank, glancing round.

'I can answer that, Frank,' said Grace, determination written all over her face. 'What we need to do now is explode not one, but *two,* cyclopes. Once and for all.'

# CHAPTER FOURTEEN

# Monsters, Monsters and more Monsters!

It was dusk by the time Grace and Danni left the House by the River. Max walked with them to the front gate, while Frank waved his fork from the door.

Max looked at the girls. 'Don't forget, if Mr Harris has regenerated once, he's highly likely to do the same thing again. I assume, when he explodes, that he reappears back in Monster World but, as we can't get there, we are just going to have to wait for him to pop back up here. So let's keep checking the Monster Scanner and Monster Radar for any changes in location for him and Neville. You've got the secure video phone from the office, haven't you? Just contact me whenever you need to, okay?'

'Max?' said Grace quietly. 'Can I ask you one more thing before we go?'

'Of course – anything,' he said kindly.

'Do you think Neville or Mr Harris might know what happened to Mum and Dad?' she asked.

Max paused, then said, 'Quite possibly. At the time they disappeared, there weren't many other cyclopes in the area, so I suspect that one of the Harrises knows something.'

'Do you think they're dead?' Grace blurted out.

Max's expression softened. 'I honestly don't know, Grace. In the game of monster-hunting, as you well know, almost anything can happen. I understand how important it is to you to find out what happened to your mum and dad. It is to me too, but you can't risk your own safety. We'll find a way to get to the bottom of what happened, I promise, but we'll do it together. Okay?'

'Okay, thank you, Max,' said Grace.

Danni smiled. 'Yes, thanks for everything, Max. We're so glad we're not on our own.'

Max smiled warmly. 'So am I. I'm here for whatever you need. But don't forget, outside this house, I'm Clive. *Clive . . .*' He looked over the girls' shoulders and raised his hand. 'Good evening, Bertram!'

'Evening, Mr Hudson,' said a chubby, grey-haired man in rainbow-coloured wellington boots, waving back from a neighbour's garden across the road. He was picking up rose clippings from the ground and putting them in a wheelbarrow.

'Nearly done for the day?' asked Max. 'You've been there morning, noon and night these past couple of weeks!'

'Aye!' Bertram agreed. 'Got to make the most of the good weather and the light evenings.'

Max gave Bertram a thumbs-up and waved again.

'Gardener, nice chap,' whispered Max.

'Although he's gone a bit welly mad these last couple of weeks – he's worn a different pair every day, I think. And you should see what he's done with the roses just lately – they're extraordinary. Anyway, that's not important! Girls, thank you for coming. It really has been wonderful to see you. And you know where I am if you need anything at all.'

Grace spent the remainder of the weekend checking the cyclopes' profiles every half an hour or so. Neville's told them much of what they already knew, along with a few new, interesting facts.

**Name**: Neville Adolphus Quentin Timothy Artemis Clarence Harris
**Type**: Cyclops
**Age**: Approximately 491
**Height**: 1.90 metres
**Weight**: 220 lbs

**Strengths**: 9 detected: shape-shifting, hypnosis, super-strength (no physical contact needed), fighting skills, eyesight, sense of smell, hearing, influencing others of his kind, horticulture.

**Weaknesses**: None of note.

**Likes**: Power, status, killing for the sake of it, bicycles, pure-breed monsters, hardy perennials, stylish and colourful footwear, modern architecture.

**Dislikes**: Too many to list in full. Of note: humans, especially those with the surname Hunter, fruit pastilles, Connect 4, his grandson.

**Best form of destruction**: Unknown, due to extreme strength and skills. Likely to be very large quantities of baking powder and a sharp object to eye.

**NOTES**: Thoroughly detests almost everyone except his daughter, Gertrudetta (Gerty). Has a particular loathing for his grandson, known only as Mr Harris. *Click here for more information.*

Number one on both the 'Most Influential' list and the 'Most Dangerous' lists in *Monster Weekly* for the last 47 years.

**DO NOT APPROACH THIS MONSTER.**

But the location for both monsters stayed the same.

Location: Unknown

Grace continued to tackle more and more monsters. Danni was baking almost around the clock to ensure she had enough cakes and biscuits to explode the most dangerous ones. There was a nasty little Tripper Upper, numerous Loaf Lickers and a particularly feisty Hair Knotter. And they were just the ones that needed exploding. Grace left the milder ones alone – the Button Gobblers and the Mess Makers – as she simply didn't have time for all of them.

The following week was no better. Grace was grateful the Harrises were still absent, as she was run off her feet dealing with Slime Imps and Sock Stealers here, there and everywhere.

By Friday, the end of term, she was exhausted. She had spent the afternoon with her classmates, playing games with the Reception children. Seven of them had reported seeing monsters that very week.

'There are so many!' Grace said to Danni, flopping into a comfy chair in the seating area at the back of the bakery. 'Like a monster army.'

'Urgh,' said Danni. 'I've already got enough to do! I'm struggling to cater for all of them. I've made one hundred and twenty macarons today, forty-eight pasties, seven different cakes, and the fiddliest salted caramel tartlets you can imagine, simply because Wardrobe Lurkers like them. I can't keep up! We need to get rid of Neville and Mr Harris as fast as possible.' She wiped her hands on her apron and carried a tray of strawberry tarts over to the window for the display, which always looked beautiful and attracted customers by the dozen.

'We will. Now Max is helping, this is going to be a walk in the park,' said Grace, putting her feet up on the table, then immediately taking them down again when she saw the look on her sister's face.

Danni turned back to the window and started to carefully place the tarts, one by one, on a pretty glass cake stand. She froze. 'Oh my goodness, Grace! Come here! Quickly!'

Grace leapt up from the chair and snatched her camera from her bag, then raced over to her sister. She was just in time to see what had caused Danni's reaction. A dark-haired, muscular-looking man on a bicycle zoomed along the pavement, forcing people to jump out of his way. The speed at which he whizzed past the shop meant she had no time to snap a photograph, but that didn't stop Grace noticing the greenish tinge to his skin. His single eye, which was just visible above the sunglasses he wore, was fixed on the path ahead. A distinctive foul smell wafted through the door to the bakery.

'Neville,' Grace whispered.

# CHAPTER FIFTEEN

# A Troublesome Troll

'Excuse me!' Mr Harris yelled, pushing through a crowd of monsters gathered in the dusty street watching a yeti, wearing a top hat and a monocle, perform a mime.

The monsters grumbled and one gorgon's snakes all turned and hissed as he barged through them. A sorceress in a bright blue coat tutted. She looked familiar to Mr Harris.

'I know there's a gate here somewhere,' he muttered. 'Why can't I find it?'

He had already tried two Human World gates that he knew of, but one of the gates had been blocked by a snoring giant that even Mr Harris wasn't strong enough to move, or brave enough to wake up. The other had what looked like a mutant vampire bat hanging from it. And no monster was *that* stupid.

'It's here somewhere, I know it is,' he whined, looking down the alleyways that separated the monster shops.

He reached a fast-food restaurant, Burger Thing, which had a big iron gate blocking the passageway at the side of the building. A small, wart-covered troll in a grey bomber jacket sat cross-legged in front of it. A shiny brass badge was clipped neatly to his lapel. It read *Alan Daniels, Gate-Keeping Troll Supervisor.*

'This one!' cried Mr Harris. 'It's this one! Finally! Let me through, please.'

'No,' hissed the troll.

Mr Harris pulled himself up to his full height. 'I said, LET ME THROUGH!' he thundered.

'No,' spat the troll. 'On the orders of my master, Neville Adolphus Quentin Timothy Artemis Clarence Harris, I will *not* let you pass.' He flared the razor-sharp claws on the ends of his scaly fingers.

'Master?' Mr Harris seethed. 'Orders?'

He looked over his shoulder to check if anyone was behind him. No one. Quick as a flash, Mr Harris picked up the hideous creature by the tuft of white hair sprouting from its head and dropped it into his enormous mouth. He swallowed.

'Urgh! Like Brussels sprouts.' He coughed.

Mr Harris pushed the gate but it didn't budge. A thick chain with a padlock held it firmly in place.

'No! This is not fair!' moaned Mr Harris. 'Oh, hang on, I know!'

Mr Harris plunged his hand into his own mouth and had a good feel around. Within seconds, he pulled out the troll's grubby coat and felt inside the pockets.

'Hurrah!' he cried, dangling an enormous rusty key from his finger. 'Thanks, Troll Face!' He threw the jacket onto the ground and unlocked the gate to Human World.

# CHAPTER SIXTEEN

# Mr Harris Returns

Max's mouth moved just slightly faster than the sound of his voice on the video phone as Grace paced around the attic. She could see Frank in the background, swiping and swinging his fork through the air like a sword.

'Well, it certainly sounds like Neville,' said Max. 'Unless you were mistaken? Perhaps it wasn't a cyclops you saw. Perhaps it was just a normal, but ugly, man on his bicycle?'

'Max, he definitely had one eye in the middle of his head,' said Grace. 'He was riding a bicycle and he wasn't Mr Harris! That fits the profile.'

The computer whirred next to her, as if it was making a huge effort to find out something useful. Without warning, its blank screen burst into life.

'Max!' cried Grace, leaping off her chair. 'Mr Harris is back! It's just come up on the computer!'

'Finally!' Max said, as Frank hopped across the screen behind him with three sharp jabs of his fork. 'What's his location?'

Grace scrolled through the information, which seemed to get more detailed every time she checked the profile. Finally, she reached the last sentence.

'Oh no,' said Grace.

'What's the matter?' asked Max. 'Where is he?'

Grace paused, then said, 'He's in Regent Street.'

'Good heavens,' said Max. 'That's a busy place. He's going to be in among a lot of people. Hopefully, he's not peckish.'

Grace zoomed in on the map provided by the Monster Scanner.

'I'm afraid he seems to be in Hamleys,' she said.

'Hamleys?' Frank piped up. 'Oh my goblins! Isn't that a toy shop? We went there last Christmas, Dad.'

'Yes. The toy shop,' said Grace. 'What should we do, Max? He'll be surrounded by children. Bite-size children!'

'We get there,' said Max. 'As quickly as we possibly can.'

'I can be there in twenty minutes if I jump on a bus,' said Grace, running down the stairs.

'Let's hope he's distracted enough not to cause any trouble for the next twenty minutes. Grace, be careful, don't take any risks,' said Max. 'I'll call a taxi but it'll take a while for me to get there.'

Danni was serving customers when Grace burst in and ran behind the counter. 'Where are the *special* doughnuts?' she asked.

'Just down here,' said Danni. 'Everything okay?'

'Got a bit of an emergency!' said Grace, staring

hard at Danni. 'Mr Harris needs some doughnuts right now – he's in Hamleys!'

'Oh, man! Excuse me just for a minute, please,' said Danni to the customer at the front of the queue. She grabbed the tray of baking-powder-laden doughnuts from beneath the counter and tipped them into Grace's rucksack, along with a large tub of baking powder.

'I didn't realise you delivered,' said the lady at the counter. 'And to Hamleys! How unusual!'

'Oh, er, yes! Mr Harris is a regular and rather . . . demanding customer. But we aim to please,' said Danni.

'How lovely,' said the lady. 'I'd like some special doughnuts delivered tomorrow, actually. It's my little Monty's birthday party and all his friends are mad on doughnuts.'

Grace shot Danni a look that said 'haha!' and 'sorry' at the same time. She dropped the video phone she was still holding into her pocket and ran out of the bakery.

As the door swung shut, she heard Danni shout, 'Be careful, Grace!'

By the time she yelled back, she was halfway down the street, sprinting towards the bus that would take her to her second encounter with Mr Harris.

## CHAPTER SEVENTEEN

# Snakes and Cyclops

'Too many people,' mumbled Mr Harris, pushing through the crowds in the vast shop. 'Move, please!' he bellowed, elbowing a shop assistant out of the way and into a mountain of cuddly toys.

Mr Harris had arrived back rather abruptly. One minute he had been in an overgrown, thorny Monster World alleyway; the next, he had been back in Human World with one foot in a shop toilet. His coat was ripped at the back and his trousers were too tight now he had digested the surprisingly filling troll, but, luckily, he still had his hat and his glasses. The change of world had left him disorientated and the shop was so vast, he couldn't see how to get out.

'Where is the door?' he shouted at no one in particular.

A little girl pointed at him. 'Mummy? Is that Chewbacca?'

'Darling, don't be rude!' replied the woman with her.

'Who is he dressed up as, then? Is it the Beast?' asked the girl.

'Lucy, it's clearly Jabba the Hutt!' said a boy behind her.

Mr Harris whipped round. 'WRONG! I am Mr Harris! Now where is the door? Ooh! Snakes and Ladders! Is this a toy shop? With games? And snacks? I mean . . . children.' He sniggered. 'Oh goodie!'

Mr Harris left the terrified boy behind and strode towards a table where Snakes and Ladders was set up for customers to play. A boy and girl were sitting down, ready to start a game.

'My turn!' he shouted, tipping the boy off his seat and picking up the red playing piece. 'I'll go first!'

'That's my brother. I was playing with him!' said the girl.

'He's fine,' said Mr Harris picking the boy up off the floor and dusting him down roughly. 'You play with me, girl. Then the winner, which will be me, will play this boy.'

'I'm really good at Snakes and Ladders,' said the girl, looking slightly wary of her enormous opponent. 'I'll beat you.'

'No, you won't!' said Mr Harris, enthusiastically shaking the dice in its cup. 'You'll be rubbish! Six! Come on, loser, your go!'

Twelve ladders, ten snakes and a hairy moment (when it looked like the cyclops might lose) later, Mr Harris cheered in triumph.

'I win! I win!' he chanted. 'I told you I'd win! Right, who wants to lose next?'

## CHAPTER EIGHTEEN

# Grace vs Mr Harris

By the time Grace arrived, breathless and sweating, at Hamleys, a crowd had formed around Mr Harris with a line of excited children waiting to challenge him.

Grace approached slowly, getting her breath back.

She could actually see that he had grown. His clothes looked too tight and the greenish skin on his wrists was really quite obvious. He was wearing his hat and his glasses, and his belly protruded some distance over the waistband of his trousers. Grace couldn't bear to think about what – or who – might be in there.

She joined the back of the queue for Snakes and Ladders. She could smell him quite clearly. The poo. The cheese. And so, it seemed, could other people. Several children had their T-shirts pulled up over their noses, and one woman was waving a Lego brochure in front of her face.

It didn't take long for her to be next. Cyclops or not, Mr Harris really was remarkably good at Snakes and Ladders.

'I win again!' he shouted. 'I love this game! I am so good at it! No one can beat me! Who's next?'

Mr Harris looked up and caught Grace's eye. It took him a moment to recognise her. 'Doughnut Lady . . .'

'Hello, Mr Harris,' Grace said politely. 'I'd like to challenge you to a game of Snakes and Ladders, please.'

'Doughnut Lady,' growled Mr Harris. 'You sent me back!'

'I don't know what you're talking about. Back to where?' asked Grace, studying her nails.

'Back to the other world,' he hissed. 'I don't like it there. It slows me down. *You* slowed me down.'

'I'm sure I didn't send you back,' said Grace as she sat down opposite him. 'You got cross because I was asking you questions. I think you got yourself into such a state, you sent yourself to the other world.'

'No, I didn't!' cried Mr Harris. 'That's not possible! I can't send myself back accidentally. I never want to go back there! That's why I'm cross with you, Doughnut Lady.'

'I still think you did it yourself,' said Grace boldly. 'Think about all the other times you've ended up there – I bet you were cross those times as well. And while we're talking about it, what exactly is this other world?' she ventured.

'Too many questions,' he said, fidgeting. The plastic stool strained under his weight. 'Like last time.'

'Sorry, I'm just curious. You seem such an interesting person,' she said, emphasising the word 'person' to imply that his disguise was still beautifully intact, and remembering what she knew about cyclopes being self-important.

'I *am* interesting,' Mr Harris agreed smugly. 'But I'm still not telling you.'

'Why?' asked Grace. 'I was quite worried when you disappeared, especially as you were so excited about meeting the Prime Minister.'

'The Prime Minister,' repeated the cyclops, leaning forward. 'Oh yes, do you really know how to find the Prime Minister? Take me!'

'Not until you tell me about the other world,' demanded Grace, trying not to think about Max warning her not to take any risks.

Mr Harris paused to think, then cried, 'I know! We'll play a game of Snakes and Ladders. If you win, which you won't, I'll tell you. If I win, which I will, you take me to the Prime Minister.'

'Promise?' said Grace.

The cyclops sighed loudly. 'I *promise*.'

Grace forced a smile and offered her hand to Mr Harris for him to shake, but immediately regretted it as he thrust his hairy, green-tinged palm towards her.

CHAPTER NINETEEN

# Mr Harris Isn't Pleased

It was neck and neck for ages. Every time Grace went up a ladder, Mr Harris harrumphed loudly and muttered a sentence containing the word 'cheat' or 'cheaty'. Every time she went down a snake, he cheered madly. By the time they reached the last row of squares on the board, Grace felt quite tense. Despite the Monster Scanner information saying Mr Harris was good at keeping promises, she was very worried that, if he lost, he would go back on his word.

The last row of squares had three snakes – on 93, 95 and 99. Her blue playing piece was on 92 and Mr Harris's on 94.

He shook the dice in his enormous hands, 'Six. Six. Six. Six. Six,' he whispered into the gap by his thumb.

He flung the dice towards the board and leaned forward in anticipation.

Five.

Mr Harris let out a guttural cry. 'This dice is wrong!'

'No, it isn't,' said Grace. 'Move your counter, please.'

Mr Harris bashed and crashed his shiny red playing piece along each of the squares until he was at 99. And a snake. For a second, Grace thought he was going to grab the board and throw it across the shop.

'Don't you dare!' said Grace. 'You're being a bad loser. And you haven't even lost yet. I still have three snakes to get past to win!'

Mr Harris breathed through his nose heavily, a bit like a bull. He followed the windy snake down to number 78 and slammed his playing piece down.

'There we are,' said Grace patiently. 'Right, let's see if I can avoid a snake or two.' She shook the dice and let it go above the board. Six. 'That was lucky,' she said, moving to 98. As she leaned forward to pick up the dice for a second turn, Mr Harris grabbed it.

'Don't be cheaty, Doughnut Lady, it's my turn!' he said.

'But I threw a six,' said Grace. 'That means I get another turn, doesn't it? That's what we've been doing the whole way through the game.'

Mr Harris was very still. He threw the dice at Grace.

'Thank you,' she said, pulling off a neat catch, feeling grateful she hadn't missed it and lost an eye, given the force with which he'd thrown it at her.

She dropped it onto the board. Two.

'Oh!' Grace exclaimed. 'I win!'

For what seemed like several minutes, Mr Harris didn't move. Then, with no warning, he tipped the board game up, scattering the dice and the playing pieces across the floor.

'I've finished,' he said matter-of-factly. 'Goodbye.'

He stood up and strode away from the table.

'Hang on a minute!' Grace shouted after him, leaping to her feet.

She conveniently forgot all the promises she had made to be careful and grabbed the cyclops's sleeve.

'You don't just get to throw a game on the floor and walk off!' she blurted out. 'You owe me information!'

An idea popped into her head.

'Oh, hang on, I get it,' she said. 'You don't want to tell me about the other world because it's boring. That's fine, then. I thought you might have something interesting and important to say but, if it's boring, I don't want to know anyway.' She let go of his sleeve. 'See you later, Mr Harris. Good luck finding the Prime Minister on your own.'

# CHAPTER TWENTY

# Grace Makes a Deal

As Grace walked away from the cyclops, she reached into her bag, took out a doughnut and sank her teeth into it.

She had barely taken five steps when she heard a shout behind her.

'It's not boring!'

She closed her eyes with relief. She turned round to find him right behind her. It made her jump, even though it wasn't unexpected. The sheer size of him was startling.

'Pardon?' she asked, taking another bite of her doughnut.

'Where I go. It isn't boring. It's actually very interesting, like me,' Mr Harris said, his eyes not moving from her doughnut. 'Where did you get that?'

'This?' she said, holding it up towards him so the sugary scent wafted towards his nose. 'From my bag. I always have doughnuts. After all, I am Doughnut Lady. And speaking of names, why don't you have a fancy name, like lots of the other monst– people I've come across?'

'I don't need a fancy name!' he snapped. 'And Harris is a very famous, important name so it's enough on its own. Now, how many of those yummy doughnuts have you got?' he said, changing the subject and looking over her shoulder at her rucksack.

'A few,' Grace said.

'I want one!' he demanded.

Grace shook her head and laughed. 'And why, exactly, should I share them with you? You didn't keep your Snakes and Ladders promise, and you are being very rude. And I never share anything with rude people.'

Mr Harris frowned and murmured under his breath, 'She's so annoying . . . but I do want a doughnut.'

'Pardon?' said Grace. 'Did you just say I was annoying?'

'No!' said Mr Harris. 'I said you were . . . er, pretty! Yes, very pretty!' He patted her roughly on the head, as though she was a Labradoodle.

'Thanks,' she said. 'That's much less rude.'

'Good. Doughnut, please!' the cyclops shouted. He grinned and gave Grace a close-up look at the width of his mouth. She could have climbed in quite comfortably.

She handed a doughnut to him. He snatched it and threw the whole thing into his gigantic gullet.

'Your doughnuts are yummy,' he said. 'Did you say you have more?'

Grace nodded. 'Yes, I have, but I'm not giving

any to you until you tell me what I'd like to know.'

Mr Harris scowled. 'Fine. You can ask me three questions. Then you give me another doughnut. Then I've got to find the Prime Minister.'

'Okay. Let's find somewhere a bit quieter than outside Hamleys to talk. Where are you going to find Prime Minister Attwood? We could speak on the way,' said Grace, starting to formulate a plan.

'The Houses of Parliament. Obviously,' said Mr Harris, tutting to emphasise Grace's stupidity.

'And how are you getting to the Houses of Parliament? It's quite a long walk.'

'I like bicycles,' he said, 'and there are lots just down here. Come on, you walk too slowly.'

Mr Harris plucked Grace off the ground and held her under his arm, like a roll of carpet. He strode off at quite a pace.

Grace couldn't decide whether to scream or throw up from the smell of Mr Harris's armpit.

As she travelled horizontally, she wondered what she must look like to passers-by, folded under the arm of an enormous man with slightly green skin. She thought if she saw someone in the same predicament, she would probably call the police, but most people barely gave her a second look.

During their strange stroll, Mr Harris used her

head as a battering ram twice, once to nudge an old lady out of the way, and then to shield his own body from someone pushing a double buggy.

He dumped Grace on her feet by a bicycle docking station, where anyone could hire a bike to get around London. The cyclops tutted, mumbled something about the bikes being 'rubbish', wrenched one out of its secure stand and hopped on.

'Quickly, please!' he said. 'Sit behind me and hold on. You can ask me three questions on the way and then I want my doughnut.'

'Fine,' said Grace. As she clambered awkwardly onto the back of the bike, which already seemed to be straining under the weight of her smelly, pedalling chauffeur, she pressed the 'connect' button on the video phone in her pocket.

She made sure her voice was loud and clear when she said, 'Right then, Mr Harris, off we go to the Houses of Parliament!'

# CHAPTER TWENTY-ONE

# What Did You Do, Mr Harris?

'First, I want to know where you go when you explode. What, exactly, is the other world?' shouted Grace as they hurtled past cars and buildings. For a very large creature, Mr Harris was a remarkably fast pedaller.

'For goodness' sake!' spat the cyclops. 'It's just the other world! Monster World!'

'As Max thought,' muttered Grace then, louder, she said, 'And, just to check, that is quite literally a world full of monsters?'

Mr Harris sighed dramatically. 'No, it's full of kittens . . . of course monsters, it's called

MONSTER WORLD! Come on, Doughnut Lady, where's your brain?'

'And when you come back from Monster World, do you always come back to the same place?' she asked.

'Yes, here!' he exclaimed.

'London?'

He shook his head in disgust. 'Where are we now?'

'London!' she replied.

'So what's the answer to your question?' he asked patronisingly.

'London.'

'Well done, thicko,' Mr Harris said rudely.

Grace chose to ignore him. 'But where in London? Always the same location?'

'Just LONDON,' he whined. 'Sometimes here, sometimes there, but I'm very good at coming back to where I want to be. Anyway, this is boring. Next question!' He swerved just in time to avoid a double-decker bus.

'Last time I saw you, in the Houses of

Parliament, you said I looked like someone you know. Who was it?' demanded Grace.

'Don't know her name. And I told you, she was annoying and so was the man she was with,' said Mr Harris.

'Can you tell me anything about her? Anything? What did her clothes look like? What about the man?' asked Grace, trying to keep the desperation out of her voice.

'That's TOO MANY questions!' said Mr Harris. 'You're cheating again!'

'Please,' said Grace, 'just tell me what you remember. If you tell me, I'll give you *two* doughnuts.'

'Fine!' cried Mr Harris. 'I can't remember much, but she had a blue coat, and the man was tall. And loud. There you are. Doughnuts, please!'

Grace swallowed hard. Her mum had always worn a peacock-blue coat. It was distinctive and beautiful and the colour was the thing that reminded Grace of her mum the most. She had especially loved the real peacock feather brooch pinned to the left lapel. Grace could almost feel its silkiness on her fingers now. It would have been easier, mind you, had she not been clinging to the back of a cyclops's scruffy tweed jacket.

'What about jewellery? Was there anything on the coat, like a decoration?' she asked.

'Nope,' said Mr Harris. 'Just a yucky feather that tickled my throat. Very annoying.'

Grace felt her blood run cold.

'Did you *eat* the woman with the blue coat?' she asked, refusing to give in to the tears prickling the backs of her eyes.

'No.'

'You're lying!'

'Fine. I was hungry. And they were right there!' the cyclops blurted out.

'You ate both of them?' Grace whispered. A sob escaped from her throat.

'Don't cough on the back of my neck while I'm trying to pedal!' snapped Mr Harris. 'And I did, but the woman is fine.'

'What do you mean? How can either of them be fine if you ate them, you vile creature?' Grace screamed.

'I know she's fine because now I'm thinking about it, I saw her today, when I was in Monster World, watching that yeti mime thing!' shouted Mr Harris. 'NOW, NO MORE QUESTIONS! You cheated me into more than three. You are *so* cheaty!' He was pedalling so fast, Grace thought the wheels might actually come off the bike.

Grace struggled to understand what she was hearing. 'You just said you saw her today? In Monster World? That's not possible!' She bashed him on the back with her fist in frustration. He didn't notice.

'Of course it is,' he spat. 'Us cyclo– cyclists have very good memories, thank you very much! And it was definitely her. She tutted at me in an annoying way. NO MORE QUES –'

Grace was forced violently forwards as Mr Harris slammed on the brakes. It was only his vastness, right in front of her, that stopped her from flying over the handlebars.

'Bad driving!' he bellowed at the black taxi they were now sitting face to face with. The driver honked his horn in one long continuous screech and Grace could hear muffled voices coming from inside. She peered around Mr Harris and saw they were just a stone's throw away from the Houses of Parliament.

As the sun went behind a cloud, the reflection on the taxi's windscreen dulled, revealing a man in the back, leaning forward, his eyes fixed on Mr Harris. Grace wondered if it was the greenish skin on show or the sheer size of him that was most bothersome to the poor passenger. All of a sudden, the man's eyes moved and locked on to her.

'Grace?' he mouthed.

'Oh,' she mouthed as she raised one hand and waved. 'Hi, Max.'

## CHAPTER TWENTY-TWO

# Doughnutty Cyclops Spit

'Grace!' Max exclaimed as he leapt out of the taxi, Frank right behind him. He dropped some money through the window. 'What on earth is happening?'

'Hi . . . Dad!' she exclaimed, widening her eyes at Max and praying he would play along.

'Mr Doughnut Lady?' said Mr Harris, eyeing Max suspiciously then looking at Frank. 'And who is this tiny, frightened child?'

Max straightened himself and looked at the cyclops. 'Good afternoon, Mr Harris,' he said. 'I'm, er, Grace's dad, and this is Frank, my son.'

Mr Harris said nothing for what seemed a long time, and then said quietly, 'Doughnut Lady's dad . . . Doughnut Lady's brother . . . How? You look nothing like each other.' He waved a meaty hand towards Frank. 'This child is so . . . puny. And what's that in his hand? For a minute I thought it was a troll's fork, all gold and fancy, but that would be ridiculous. How would a child that feeble be important enough to have a troll's fork? They never give decent forks away, only cheap things!' He laughed raucously at the thought. 'And you, Mr Doughnut Lady,' Mr Harris went on, pointing at Max, 'how did you know my name?'

'Because I've talked about you!' Grace interjected. 'Like I told you before, you're interesting, *and* you exploded, so I told my dad about you.'

Mr Harris smiled a grotesque smile.

Max nodded. 'She did. But, may I ask, Mr Harris, where are you and . . . my daughter going?'

'To see the Prime Minister,' said Mr Harris gleefully. 'I need to *m-eat* her!' He snorted with laughter. Frank whimpered and raised his fork defensively.

'Oh, right, that sounds important. And why are you accompanying Mr Harris?' Max turned to Grace.

Mr Harris interrupted rudely. 'Because she knows the Prime Minister, so I don't need an appointment.'

Grace nodded, her eyes pleading with Max to go along with her story. She glanced at Frank reassuringly.

'And I've brought some of Mrs Attwood's favourite doughnuts that she asked for,' said Grace.

Mr Harris whipped round. 'What about *my* doughnuts?'

Grace delved into her bag and held one up. 'Here, have one now.'

Mr Harris snatched it and dropped it into his mouth. 'Yum! You should eat more of these, Doughnut Lady's shrimp of a brother – you could do with fattening up,' he said, spraying Frank with doughnutty cyclops spit.

'She certainly does make good doughnuts,' agreed Max, producing a handkerchief from his jacket pocket and wiping Frank's cheek.

'I want my other one,' said Mr Harris abruptly. 'You promised me two.'

Grace handed him another.

'I'll eat it on the way,' said Mr Harris, striding off.

Grace and Max hurried after him, with Frank just about keeping up behind them, his fork clutched tightly in his hand.

## CHAPTER TWENTY-THREE

# Bang! Again

'Oh my goblins! He wants to f-fatten me up!' cried Frank. 'He's planning to eat me! I remember exactly what the Monster Scanner notes say – tendency to eat p-people with little or no warning! His danger score is 100!'

'Frank, he really isn't planning that, you wouldn't fill him up at all,' Max gabbled. 'Grace, what's going on? Are you friends with him? Were you on his bike?!'

'I'm absolutely *not* friends with him,' replied Grace. 'I had to go with him to get him talking, and because I couldn't explode him in the middle of a toy shop. And it was worth it, Max. I got information!'

'Was it information about him wanting to eat m-me?' stuttered Frank.

'Hurry up!' shouted Mr Harris from in front of them.

Grace looked ahead to the visitors' entrance. There were several security guards.

'We're not going in that way today,' she said. 'We're going to the special entrance at the side.'

'We can't actually go inside!' Max whispered.

'We won't,' Grace replied. 'We'll explode him out here, out of sight.'

The little colour left in Frank's cheeks drained away. 'Explode him? I think I might be sick.'

'You said you got information?' Max said hurriedly.

'Yes! Max, you won't believe this, but he ate Mum and Dad! And he says he's seen Mum in Monster World since – so it's possible she, or even both of them, might still be alive. I haven't had

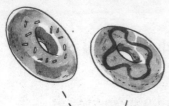

the chance to ask him anything about Neville yet, but there might still be time.'

Max stood open-mouthed. Frank gagged.

'Where's this special entrance?' said Mr Harris. 'Come on, Doughnut Lady and Mr Doughnut Lady and tiny shrimp boy, I haven't got all day!'

'It's round here,' said Grace, leading Mr Harris, Max and Frank to the door of a building at the side of the main Houses, which said *Staff Only*.

Mr Harris lurched towards the door.

'Are you really going to go in looking like that?' Grace blurted, as her brain worked at lightning speed to come up with a plan to delay him – and explode him. 'You're meeting the Prime Minister and you're a mess! And by the way, I've found another doughnut.'

'Grace,' Max warned her quietly. 'I wouldn't push your luck . . .'

'Grace, don't!' cried Frank,

tugging on her rucksack, trying to pull her back.

She mouthed, 'Trust me.'

'Doughnut!' said Mr Harris, holding out his giant hand.

'Here,' said Grace. 'Now, eat it slowly while I dust off your jacket. Did you know it's ripped at the back?' As she chatted, she took the opportunity to sprinkle baking powder across his shoulders.

Mr Harris didn't reply. He ate his doughnut slowly. Slowly, that is, for a man-eating cyclops.

'There,' she said. 'Much better.'

She gave a thumbs-up behind her back so Max and Frank could see, while holding the tub of powder in the other hand in case what she had already used wasn't enough.

'Right, well, given that you probably won't be hanging around, I might as well take the chance to ask. Mr Harris, do you know where your grandfather, Neville Harris, is? We need to know!' Grace blurted.

Mr Harris whipped around to face her. 'How

do you know him? And why would I know where he is? He's scum!'

'We're pretty sure he's nearby. If you have any idea where, you need to tell us now! He's dangerous, and there's every chance he's going to get to the Prime Minister before you do!' exclaimed Grace.

Mr Harris let out a menacing growl and lifted Grace up by her backpack.

Frank yelped and Max put his arm protectively in front of him.

'Mr Harris, put her down and listen! We know that Neville is close, and if you would just calm down, maybe you could help us work out where he is, so we can destroy him,' said Max.

'You can't *destroy* him! I'm the only one who can do that. He's mine!' snarled the cyclops, lifting Grace higher.

'Put me down now!' she demanded, face to face with the cyclops. 'This is hurting my arms and your breath stinks!'

He looked at Max, breathing heavily through his nose. 'Your daughter is VERY rude.'

'This is too dangerous, Grace!' Max yelled. 'Do it now!'

Grace used her thumb to flick the lid off the tub of baking powder and threw the contents at Mr Harris's face. Some went directly into his mouth.

The cyclops suddenly became very still. He let go of Grace, who dropped to the ground.

'Doughnut Lady, was that breath freshener? I feel funny. What have you done?' he said. He swiped a beefy arm towards Grace but, at the same time, shot backwards, spinning, until he was no more than a speck in the distance.

# CHAPTER TWENTY-FOUR

# Frank's Masterpiece

Back at Cake Hunters, Grace and Danni found Frank a blanket and made him a sugary mug of hot chocolate. Max had returned to Henley immediately after Mr Harris's explosion, to speak to the Prime Minister's office. Frank had been happy to go back to the bakery with Grace and wait for him there. While the hot chocolate cooled, he built a fort out of a table and three chairs and was making notes inside it, fork in one hand, pen in the other.

Danni was busy making iced buns exactly the way Tripper Uppers liked them, due to another

surge in sightings. As she bustled in in a cloud of icing sugar, Grace explained what had happened at Hamleys, then at the Houses of Parliament. Well, most of what had happened.

'So, there's a chance Mum could still be alive. Mr Harris says he *saw* her! Maybe Dad is still alive too,' she finished, unable to keep the hope from her voice.

Danni frowned. 'Maybe, but we can't be absolutely sure that what Mr Harris is said is right, or the truth. And even if he is right, how on earth do we get them back from Monster World?'

'Mr Harris will come back. He's a regenerator. You could ask him how to do it, Grace. You're brave enough. Although it would be very dangerous,' said Frank, looking out between the slats of an upturned chair.

'I don't mind the danger too much, but I'm not sure he'll want to tell me after I exploded him again. But I'll come up with something,' Grace replied. 'And don't worry about any of it, Frank. We'll come up with a really good plan when your dad gets here. Now you've seen that we can explode him, you know it'll all be fine.'

'I suppose so,' said Frank. 'I thought he was going to eat all of us when you mentioned N-Neville.' He held his fork a little higher. It was trembling.

'He'd have eaten me ages ago if that's what he was planning,' said Grace. 'It's annoying that he doesn't know where Neville is. We've got to find him. He's bound to try and get to the Prime Minister before Mr Harris does.'

'But if either of them get to the Prime Minister, what are they going to do?' asked Danni as she measured and mixed ingredients. 'They can't just eat her and take over, cyclops or not.'

'Both would probably try!' exclaimed Frank. 'Mr Harris would eat the Prime Minister in one big gulp, and Neville's profile says he can shape-shift, so he could be anywhere. And we know how many monster sightings there have been. Dad says they're an army. And Dad is the best monster-hunter there is . . . apart from you. And your mum and dad.' Frank looked at the floor at the mention of the girls' parents.

Danni smiled and put a batch of buns into the oven. 'You're right, Frank, he is the best monster-hunter there is. He knows so much.'

'He's teaching me,' said Frank, 'but I'll never be as b-brave as he is. Or Grace. I've never exploded a m-monster before. Today was the first time I'd been near a really d-dangerous one.'

'Well, then you're already really brave,' said Danni.

Grace nodded. 'You are. Mr Harris is a pretty serious monster for your first encounter.'

'But you even told him off when he had lifted you up off the ground! I would have screamed!' exclaimed Frank.

'You did what?' demanded Danni, looking at Grace.

'Oh, nothing!' Grace said quickly. 'Don't worry about that. Frank, tell us more about what you've learned from Max.'

'W-well, I have a good memory so I'm learning all about the different types of monster. I remember quite a few from M-Monster World too,' Frank said.

'Of course!' said Grace. 'How much do you remember about your time there, Frank? That is, if you don't mind talking about it?'

'I don't mind. Now I'm safe with Dad,' said Frank, half in and half out of his fort. 'My goblin mum was quite nice but my goblin dad was a bit scary. They told me they found me outside a bowling alley when I was a baby, but I don't think that's true.'

'What's it like in Monster World?' asked Danni.

Frank shuddered. 'It's not good. There are so many different monsters everywhere. Even the trees and bushes are weird and scary, and the buildings are all different shapes and sizes. The food is disgusting, which is probably why they all like your cakes so much.'

'Thank goodness Max found you,' said Grace.

'I know,' said Frank, nodding. 'He's promised I'll never have to go back there, even with my future monster-hunting duties.'

'With your amazing office, you can monster-hunt from the comfort of your own home,' said Danni. 'And speaking of monster-hunting, should we check the Monster Scanner again for Neville?'

'Yep,' Grace said. 'Actually, Frank, do you think you could draw him? Perhaps a better, clearer version of that photo you have? If we use a picture as well as his name, it might come up with more information. It's always better with both and it seems to have been struggling with his location, mainly because of the shape-shifting, so a picture could really help.'

'I can try,' said Frank, looking worried. He picked up the pencil he had been making notes with and began to sketch. He seemed to go into a world of his own. His hand flew across the paper wildly and he spoke quietly to himself. Grace couldn't hear much of what he said, other than the odd word – ugly, mean, pointy, green.

After a couple of minutes, Frank put the pencil down and handed the paper to Grace.

'Frank, this drawing is brilliant!' said Grace. 'Let's get it into the Monster Scanner. What are we waiting for?'

'Actually, buns and cookies,' replied Danni. 'Sorry, three more minutes then we can all go up to the attic.'

Frank looked worried. 'I don't like attics much. But I do like cookies. What sort are you making, Danni?'

Danni scrunched her nose. 'Sorry – they're peanut butter and Marmite,' she said. 'A Sock Stealer's absolute favourite.'

'Urgh!' said Frank.

'Sock Stealers have really bad taste,' said Danni. 'But I've also made a Victoria sponge for the Milk Drinkers, lemon drizzle muffins for the Messer Uppers and *mille-feuille* for the Snot-nosed Ogres – they love French patisserie.'

'That's a lot of cakes,' said Frank. 'Don't you have to make human ones too?'

Grace grinned. 'She's mixed them up a few times.'

Danni blushed. 'Mr Johnson was not at all keen on the broccoli macarons I gave him accidentally, instead of the pistachio ones.'

Frank giggled.

'Vegetable Nibblers love the broccoli ones,' said Danni, as the timer on the oven pinged. 'But Mr Johnson really didn't.'

'Right,' said Grace, pushing her chair away from the table, 'Monster Scanner time.'

## CHAPTER TWENTY-FIVE

# Attack!

Grace studied Frank's sketch of the muscular, one-eyed creature. He had dark, slicked-back, greasy-looking hair and pointy, almost snake-like, features. His almond-shaped eye looked piercing and evil, and his mouth was wide, like Mr Harris's, although his gullet didn't look nearly as bulbous.

'Okay, well, here goes,' said Grace as she placed the drawing inside the Monster Scanner. She, Danni and Frank were crammed into the tiny attic space like sardines in a tin. They watched the Monster Scanner screen intently, waiting for

the results. It didn't take long. Neville's profile popped back up.

Grace scanned it. 'Shape-shifting . . . likes power . . . footwear . . . hates his grandson . . . fruit pastilles . . . no one hates fruit pastilles! Most influential . . . dangerous . . . intelligence 95. There's nothing new here!' she said, frustrated. 'Violence 100, danger 100 plus – yep, we know this already.'

'Oh my goblins! Look, Grace,' Frank piped up. 'Look at the location.'

Grace scanned down the screen.

**Location**: Henley-on-Thames
**Previous locations within last 24 hours**: London – Downing Street, Westminster, Camden, Columbia Road Flower Market.

'Henley!' they all said at once.

'Dad!' cried Frank. He gestured wildly with his fork in the direction he seemed to think Henley was in.

'Don't worry, Frank, we'll call him now. He will be absolutely fine,' said Danni calmly, giving Frank's shoulder a reassuring squeeze without getting too near the pointy end of his fork.

Grace grabbed the video phone and hit the 'redial' button. It only rang once before Max answered it. His face took up most of the screen.

'Dad!' shouted Frank. 'Are you okay? Are you at home? NEVILLE'S IN HENLEY!'

'Shhh!' whispered Max. 'Keep your voice down. Something here is not quite right.'

'What do you mean?' Grace asked urgently, keeping her voice low.

'I've just seen Bertram, the gardener. He's trying to get into the house through the French doors. I'm not sure he's who we think he is,' Max breathed, his eyes darting from side to side.

Grace replied quietly, 'Max, listen, Neville appears to be in Henley. We've just seen it on the Monster Scanner. Do you think he could be linked to Bertram somehow?'

'Dad! What's going on?' Frank whisper-shouted into the video phone. 'Have you phoned the Prime Minister? Why do you think Bertram's not Bertram?'

'Frank, don't worry, it'll be fine,' said Max reassuringly. 'I've phoned the Prime Minister's office and they're sending a car for me now.

I'll be back at the bakery to get you before you can say "Dad deserves more cakes"!'

Frank smiled nervously. 'Okay. Dad deserves more –'

A crash behind Max interrupted Frank. The video phone jolted downwards, showing two pairs of shoes: Max's brown brogues and a pair of red, shiny wellington boots. They were locked in a stance that suggested a struggle was taking place. The phone continued to lurch and zoom until it fell with a crack to the ground. The screen went grainy and then blank.

'Max?' shouted Grace. 'MAX?'

# CHAPTER TWENTY-SIX

# Tasty Trolls

'What? Again? She has! She's done it again! I knew it was her,' hissed Mr Harris as he landed in Monster World, on his bottom, right outside Burger Thing and a bakery called Cookie Monsters. 'How can someone so small be so annoying!' He let out a snarl of anger as he took in his surroundings. 'Oh! But at least I'm near a Human World gate. Argh, for goodness' sake, there's another warty troll. Here we go again . . .'

As Mr Harris heaved himself to his feet, a row of delicious-looking doughnuts in the window of Cookie Monsters caught his eye.

'Ooh, yum,' he said. 'They look just like Doughnut Lady's doughnuts. I've probably got time for a couple. I won't be long. They'll make the troll taste better.'

He pushed open the bakery door and, seeing a familiar bright blue coat, said, 'Ah, Blue Coat Lady, you work here! One double doughnut surprise, please.'

## CHAPTER TWENTY-SEVEN

# Bertram

Grace, Danni and Frank crept down the path towards the House by the River, all three of them clutching pots of baking powder firmly in their hands. Grace was at the front and Danni at the back, with Frank sandwiched between them, his fork grasped in his free hand.

'You should've let me come on my own,' whispered Grace to Danni. 'We shouldn't all be here.'

'Not a chance,' Danni replied, scanning the area around them intensely. 'Although I have to admit that this is a bit out of my comfort zone.

Do I literally just lob this stuff?' She held up the baking powder.

'I've got a w-weak throw,' Frank said quietly.

'Hopefully, neither of you will have to throw anything,' said Grace, tucking her catapult into the pocket of her jeans, just in case. 'Let's go round to the back.'

They edged silently round the side of the house, peering warily around. The garden was eerily still.

'Look!' Danni gasped.

At the back, the beautiful Victorian house was L-shaped, so they could easily see into the kitchen through the French doors from the opposite corner of the building. Max was tied to a chair in the middle of the room. His hair was messy and his shirt crumpled.

Another man came into view, his back to them. He was grey-haired and chubby, and wearing bright red wellington boots.

'Bertram!' whispered Grace.

'What's he doing?' wailed Frank. 'Why has he tied Dad up?'

They watched as Bertram circled Max, bending down close to his face, speaking and sneering. Suddenly, he raised one arm above Max's head.

'Grace! We have to do something!' cried Frank.

'Shhh.' Grace put her arm around Frank's trembling shoulders. She could see how worried he was about Max and she felt a brief pang of sadness for her own eccentric, gangly, good-humoured dad.

At the same moment, Bertram became very still and, with no warning, whipped round to look through the French doors. He cupped his eyes and moved nearer the glass, sniffing the air like a dog.

The girls and Frank shuffled backwards, out of view, holding their breath.

'What do we do?' mouthed Danni.

'Nothing for now,' breathed Grace, holding

her baking powder at shoulder height, her arm poised, ready to strike.

Danni nodded nervously. She and Frank copied Grace's stance.

After what seemed like an age of silence, Grace edged forward very slowly, hunched down, and glanced round the corner. She was just in time to see Bertram raise his arm again. But rather than thump it down, he daintily plucked a hair from Max's head.

Grace didn't need to be a lip reader to know that Max responded with, 'Ow! You idiot!'

Bertram threw his head back and laughed. Then he dangled the hair above his face and dropped it into his mouth.

'Is he *eating* it?' said Danni, who was looking over the top of Grace's head.

'I think he is,' said Grace, bewildered.

Frank, who was on his knees by the girls, screwed up his face in disgust.

They watched as Bertram chewed steadily.

With every crunch of his jaw, his body seemed to pulse. All at once, his piercing blue eyes merged into one big yellow eye in the middle of his head, his grey hair turned black and greasy, and his chubby body transformed into a tall, muscular form.

'Neville!' All three of them whispered the name. At the same time, they saw Max mouth the name in the kitchen.

'Bertram isn't linked to Neville!' exclaimed Grace. 'He *is* Neville!'

'Shape-shifting,' said Frank. 'Remember his profile!'

Neville's forked tongue flicked one last time as he swallowed the hair, and immediately he transformed again. This time, into Max.

They watched in horror as Neville, looking just like Max, picked up the chair, with Max still on it, and shot towards the French doors. He carried Max as if he weighed nothing at all, in one hand, and slid the door open with the other. He raced across the garden, elbowed open the door to the potting shed, and threw Max and the chair inside. With no hesitation, he ran noiselessly back across the garden and round the other side of the house. In the distance, a car door closed and there was the rumble of a car engine moving off down the road.

'Dad!' Frank shrieked and raced forward.

'Max!' Grace blurted, speeding across the lawn towards the potting shed, Danni right behind her.

# CHAPTER TWENTY-EIGHT

# Wellington Boots

Miraculously, Max and his chair had landed upright inside the potting shed. He looked more shocked to see them than he had coming face to face with Neville.

'Frank! Girls! Thank goodness! I can't believe you're here!' he spluttered.

'Dad!' yelled Frank, hurling himself at Max.

'Ouch! Careful with that fork, son, I nearly lost an eye!' said Max cheerily. 'Don't be upset, Frank, I'm fine. Completely unscathed, actually. Well apart from the hair he plucked out of my head, which was surprisingly stingy.'

'Are you sure you're not hurt?' said Grace, grabbing a pair of gardening scissors and cutting through the twine that was wrapped around Max's body, securing him to the wooden chair.

'I'm fine. I'm so relieved you came! I knew something was wrong the moment I saw him sprint across the garden. He was far too fast for an elderly gardener. When he tried the handles to the French doors, his hands were pulsing – a sure sign of a shape-shifter. Then I saw the super-shiny wellies, remembered the mention of footwear in Neville's profile, and *bam!* I knew I was in trouble. He got in while I was on the call with you. He overpowered me in seconds. He's like a juggernaut!'

'And now he's shape-shifted into you!' cried Danni.

Max nodded gravely.

Grace bent down to cut the twine securing Max's ankles to the chair legs. As the string pinged away, she noticed a pair of rainbow wellington boots tucked into the far corner of the potting shed. Grace ran over and picked them up. They were stuffed full of papers.

'Neville's other wellies,' she said. 'And look.'

She emptied the contents onto the work bench by the window. Several sheets of rolled-up paper, a red marker, a half-eaten packet of Maltesers and a copy of *Monster Weekly* rolled out. Grace hastily unrolled the papers.

'Wow,' she murmured, staring at a list of hundreds of what could only be monster names. 'These must be the ones on his side who've shifted over to here from Monster World. They have ticks next to them, and some even have locations and mobile numbers. Look – Esmerelda Esperanta, Hertfordshire, phone number, tick. Arthur Barty-Smith the Second, Glasgow, email address, tick. Razor McClawface, Cornwall, phone and email, tick. He doesn't sound great.'

'The McClawfaces are werewolves, they're very bitey,' said Max.

'The McClawfaces are a massive f-family,' said Frank. 'I went to a Monsterssori nursery with the McClawface twins when I was in M-Monster World. It wasn't good. They brought in live rats for snack-time.'

Max ruffled Frank's hair.

'He's got the whole country covered!' exclaimed Danni. 'Look! Bristol, Sheffield, Manchester, Liverpool, Canterbury, York – even the Isle of Wight is on there!'

Grace lifted the page up to glance at the one underneath.

'Oh!' said Danni, Frank and Max at the same time as the page revealed itself to be a montage of photos, showing the Prime Minister, the famous front door of 10 Downing Street, and a range of patterned, colourful wellington boots. A pair of particularly awful gold ones had been circled with the red marker, with a heart scrawled next to them. Newspaper print letters of different sizes had been cut out and stuck onto the paper to spell out 'Hunter Family'. Worryingly, Neville had scrawled 'EXTERMINATE!' over the top of them.

The sheets underneath contained a wealth of information Neville had managed to get his hands on. There were maps, blueprints of 10 Downing Street, a photo of the front of Cake Hunters, several pictures of Max entering and leaving the House by the River, a receipt from a local shoe shop for a pair of striped wellington boots, a packet of 'Russian Giant' sunflower seeds, a photocopy of Mr Harris's Monster Scanner profile, and several articles about the Prime Minister. There were also copious notes in what Grace assumed to be Neville's handwriting, which was surprisingly neat.

'He's headed for the Prime Minister. We need to go,' said Max seriously.

'Now?' asked Frank, wide-eyed.

Max nodded. 'There's a murderous cyclops on his way to Downing Street, looking exactly like me and travelling in my official government car. I think now is the only option.'

## CHAPTER TWENTY-NINE

# Mr Harris Causes a Scene

Grace and Danni hurried alongside Max, who was on the phone to the head of the Prime Minister's security team, as they walked into the throng of people jostling in every direction towards Downing Street.

After Max had returned his phone to his pocket, he put his hand protectively on Frank's shoulder and said, 'It's not good. I'm already there, apparently, waiting patiently and reading *Homes & Gardens* magazine.'

'What's the plan?' Danni asked as they moved through the crowds

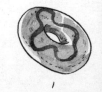

as fast as they could without knocking anyone over.

'We need to get in and get him contained in the first instance. I've told the security team not to get anywhere near him, as they won't have a clue what to do,' said Max, manoeuvring people out of their path. 'Then we need to throw everything we have at him until we can either secure and remove him or explode him. Grace, do you agree?'

'Yes,' said Grace. 'I've got plenty of equipment with me. We'll do whatever it takes.'

The people in front of them had slowed down until they were barely able to shuffle forward. Max craned his neck. 'Oh come on, what's going on here?'

A wall of people blocked the pavement. They were clearly looking at something.

'Excuse me,' Max shouted, pushing through, 'please move aside. We're on government business.'

'Well, you might want to sort this out then,' a voice from the crowd piped up. 'The big bloke is a right troublemaker.'

Grace stood on tiptoe to get a better look.

There, standing on the pavement, dressed in his now even tattier and more questionable 'normal' clothes, was Mr Harris. His glasses were wonky, meaning the fake eyes on the lenses were also wonky. His jacket sported an even larger rip and his trousers flapped wildly round his ankles, revealing a considerable portion of green-tinged skin. His hat was at a jaunty angle on his enormous head.

'It's rude to stare,' he spat at his crowd of onlookers.

'For goodness' sake! He's back again,' whispered Grace.

'His timing is extraordinary. Why chuck one cyclops at us when we could be dealing with two?' said Max. He addressed the crowd. 'Move on, please, there's nothing to see here. I have it all under control. Government business! That's it, move on now.'

Grace watched as people started to move away, bored now it looked as if no one would be punched on the nose by a remarkably large, ugly man in a grotty tweed jacket.

She turned to where Mr Harris was standing, to see he was staring right at her, his arms folded across his huge chest. He didn't look pleased.

'Mr Harris,' she said, fighting off a tiny surge of something she had not expected. Was it excitement?

'You threw exploding powder into my mouth just as I was about to meet the Prime Minister,' he said.

'I'm sorry, but I had to,' Grace said. 'You were getting very shouty and aggressive.'

'Well, that's *your* fault,' said Mr Harris,

jabbing a meaty finger towards her. 'Why you had to start talking about my grandfather, I don't know.'

Grace rolled her eyes. 'I had to check if you knew where he was and what he was up to. As it happens, *we* now know all of that ourselves anyway.'

Max interjected. 'She's right, Mr Harris. You should know that Neville is, in fact, about a hundred metres down the road, looking like me and waiting to meet the Prime Minister. We believe he has plans to take over the country and lead a nation of evil monsters.'

'No!' bellowed Mr Harris. He started to stomp, at speed, towards the gate for 10 Downing Street.

# CHAPTER THIRTY

# Grace Jumps In

'Mr Harris! Stop!' shouted Grace. 'You'll never get in there without Max!'

'She's right,' called Danni bravely. 'There's maximum security and iIf you make a fuss, they'll arrest you.'

Mr Harris got back to them in one large stride. 'Get me in, then.'

Grace looked at Max. 'He might actually be able to help us with Neville.'

Max nodded. 'It's an option. But is it an option that we can trust?'

'Finally!' said Mr Harris.

'Doughnut Lady has said something sensible. Now, get me in.'

'Mr Harris,' said Grace, looking at the cyclops, 'we *will* get you in but first of all you have to promise me two things. First, I need you to promise you will not, under any circumstances, eat the Prime Minister.'

'Oh, why?' Mr Harris wailed.

'We will be going in there to save her. It would be pretty bad if we saved her and then you ate her,' said Grace. Frank nodded nervously from behind Danni.

'Then what do I get?' hissed Mr Harris.

'Well, you'll get to meet her, won't you? That's exactly what you've wanted to do all along,' said Grace. 'If you help us save Mrs Attwood, you'll be a hero, Mr Harris. Plus, surely it's a bonus to stop your grandfather? I'll even help you do it.'

Mr Harris stopped, clearly thinking. 'Oh, fine. I won't eat her. But I'm not happy about it. Let's go.'

'Not so fast! There's another promise you need

to make,' said Grace. 'There isn't time to explain properly but the lady you ate in the blue coat is my mum. If you honestly think you saw her, I really need you to promise that you'll help me rescue her from Monster World.'

Mr Harris frowned. 'So that's why you went on and on and on,' he said. 'Fine. If you're going to keep going on and on and on, then I'll try. Now, get me in. I will NOT let HIM get there before me.'

Frank wedged himself between Danni and Max, seeming to become even smaller than usual.

'Mr Harris, you'll scare Mrs Attwood,' said Grace. 'You need to calm down and tidy yourself up. Here, I'll do it, quick!' she added, keen to cover some of the greenish skin on show.

Max leaned towards Grace and whispered, 'Don't bother. He's unlikely to come out of this in one piece.'

Grace stopped. It was true. If Neville was as powerful as everyone seemed to think, the situation would probably not end well for Mr

Harris. And his demise, before he had helped her try to find her parents, would present a whole different problem. Grace's mind whirred. Not finding – or at least looking for – her parents was not an option. Then an idea came to her in a blinding flash. She knew exactly what she had to do. It was her only chance.

'Mr Harris, you have something in your teeth.' She pointed to her own to show him where.

'G-grace? Please don't get so close!' cried Frank. 'He might eat you.'

Mr Harris glared at Frank. 'Oh, Doughnut Lady, I don't care. Here?' he moaned, pointing to a massive jagged tooth at the front of his mouth.

'No, further back,' she said.

Mr Harris opened his mouth wide and felt around his back teeth.

'Oh my goblins! Grace! Please stop. I don't like the smell!'

She felt Frank tug on her cardigan. 'Bit wider!' she said.

'Grace! NO!' shouted Danni, suddenly realising what her little sister was about to do.

But before anyone could stop her, Grace leapt towards the cavernous, foul-smelling hole, tucking her knees in. Her pot of baking powder, lid off, was in her hand.

As she flew through the air, she shouted, 'I'm sorry, but I have to try! This might be our only chance to find them. Hold Neville off – we'll be back in a flash, I promise!'

## CHAPTER THIRTY-ONE

# A Family Reunion

Grace flew out of Mr Harris's giant gullet with a violent jolt. The moment she was free, he started to complain loudly.

'What did you do? You are so badly behaved! We were meant to be destroying my grandfather and you have ruined EVERYTHING! And for goodness' sake, why is *that* here?'

Grace looked behind her. Her blood ran cold. 'Frank!'

Frank's eyes were so wide, they looked like they might pop out of his head. His fork had something slimy on the end, which must have come from Mr Harris's smelly throat.

'I was h-holding on to your cardigan,' he whimpered.

Grace closed her eyes for a moment. 'I'm so sorry, Frank. But listen, you'll be fine. Just stick with me, okay? We'll be as quick as possible.'

'Doughnut Lady and small shrimp boy, I deserve an apology!' bellowed Mr Harris.

'Fine! Sorry,' snapped Grace. 'But I had no choice. I couldn't risk you deciding not to help me find my mum after we had been in 10 Downing Street.' She decided to leave out the fact that he may not have made it out of Downing Street at all.

'You've ruined it!' Mr Harris shouted. 'And you made me gag!'

'For goodness' sake,' Grace hissed. 'We will get back as soon as possible, I promise. And you had to gag so we could get out of your mouth! Anyway, you've covered us in spit! Urgh!'

Mr Harris turned his head away. 'You both stink.'

'I'm sure we do!' she cried. 'That'll be your spit! Or breath! Or both!'

She looked at Frank, who was still lying where he had landed, curled into a ball on the cobbles by her feet. She felt terrible that he had ended up away from Max and back in Monster World, a place he had said he never wanted to go back to.

Mr Harris shook his head slowly and patronisingly. 'What now? Now you've spoiled everything.'

'We find my mum.' she said, looking around properly and taking in her surroundings. The buildings were higgledy-piggledy, some tall, some tiny, some painted bright colours, some so dirty you couldn't even tell if they had windows. A small, strange-looking hairy monster, with tiny legs and a face a bit like a monkey waddled by. A Poo Shuffler! And a line of large-eared, ugly creatures, holding sticks, were moving towards them from further down the road. Grace hoped Frank hadn't noticed.

Mr Harris looked around. 'This is not where
I've seen the blue coat lady. So, can't do it. Let's
go back and I'll be a hero, et cetera.'

'Well, where was she last time you saw her?'
cried Grace.

'Here?' Mr Harris waved his arm meaninglessly.
'There?' He pointed down a bushy side road.
'I don't know!'

'Mr Harris!' yelled Grace. 'Please! Stop talking

nonsense and help me find her. If we don't get back as soon as we can, it could be too late. Your grandfather could be with the Prime Minister right now! Where do we go?'

'Back where you came from,' a voice growled from behind Grace. 'You don't look like you belong here.'

'Could be dangerous,' another voice jeered. 'For a *human*.'

Something sniffed the back of her neck. Grace moved round slowly and came face to face with one of the large-eared ugly creatures she'd seen coming down the road. It was with five others, and none of them looked friendly. They circled Grace, Mr Harris and Frank like sharks.

'Urgh, yuck, goblins,' said Mr Harris.

'Why are you here, humans?' said the biggest

and ugliest goblin, who had sharp, pointy teeth and mean lilac eyes.

'I'm not a human,' spat Mr Harris. 'I'm a cyclops.' He whipped off his glasses to reveal his real eye. Then he turned to Grace. 'You knew, yes?'

'Of course I knew!' she snapped.

'And why is a cyclops keeping company with humans?' the big goblin glowered. Then he pointed to Frank, who had hunched his face towards his knees,. 'Is this human?'

Mr Harris nodded. 'Apparently.'

The large goblin used his stick to hook the back of Frank's T-shirt and lift him off the ground. Gradually, Frank uncurled. As his face came into view, Grace could see his eyes were shut and his fork was held out in front of him.

'FRANKENSTEIN? MY BA-BY!' A hideously ugly goblin with blonde hair and a pink tutu rushed forward. 'Where have you been?'

'What?' Grace gasped.

## CHAPTER THIRTY-TWO

# Cookie Monsters

Frank opened one eye a millimetre. A hint of recognition swept over his pale face. The blonde goblin unhooked him from the stick and cradled him like a baby.

'I've missed you so much,' she crooned. 'Let's go home and I'll make you fleas on toast. Your favourite! Ripper can deal with these two.' She pointed towards the biggest goblin, then looked over to Grace and Mr Harris.

'What? How does the fancy goblin know the shrimpy sibling?' questioned Mr Harris.

Before Grace could say anything, Frank looked

at her, gave a barely noticeable nod and took a deep breath. 'Mummy?'

The blonde goblin beamed with pride. 'Yes, my darling Frankensteiny-weiny . . .'

Mr Harris baulked. 'Mummy? Frankensteiny-weiny? Doughnut Lady, what on earth is going on? Is that thing your mum as well? Are you part goblin? I knew it, you've got such an attitude. Now it all makes sense.'

'NOT NOW,' Grace said in a shouty whisper.

The tutu'd goblin was waiting expectantly for Frank to speak.

'C-can my friends come home with us, please?' he asked.

'Oh. Well, if it makes my baby happy, then okay. Ripper, leave the other two for now,' she said, tickling Frank's tummy with her long claws, which were painted with sparkly purple nail varnish.

Ripper looked at them menacingly and drew one spiky finger across his throat as a warning.

Mr Harris looked at Grace and stifled a giggle. 'Like he could hurt me! You? Yes, you'd be dead in a second,' he said. 'But me? Not a chance!'

Grace and Mr Harris were led down a side road by the six goblins, who were all so delighted by Frank's return to Monster World, they took it in turns to carry him. Although Frank was holding it together and seemed remarkably calm, Grace knew how terrified he really was from the way his fork jerked and twitched every few seconds. She had to keep him safe.

They walked through a maze of narrow, dusty roads until the space opened out and shops lined the sides of the street. There were clothes shops with the most bizarre selections of clothes Grace had ever seen, toy shops, shoe shops (selling any number of shoes at a time for several-legged monsters), book shops, even a mobile phone shop. Cafés boasted the day's 'specials' – gloop of the day, live worm bolognaise and mice cream. There was even a fast-food restaurant called

Burger Thing. Grace had never seen anything like it. Well, she hadn't until she saw the window of the shop next to Burger Thing. It was a bakery – Cookie Monsters. She slowed, mesmerised. If it hadn't been for the frog's legs poking out of the top of a muffin, and the giant millipede wrapped round a wedding cake like a ribbon, she could

have been outside her own bakery. It looked so similar. It was painted yellow, just like Cake Hunters, and the window display was as beautiful as those her mum had taught Danni to replicate.

It would have been more beautiful without the maggots used as sprinkles and the cockroaches in the pecan brittle, but still . . .

'Oh!' said Mr Harris. 'This is the place.'

'What place?' Grace asked.

'The place with the blue coat lady you say is your mum. Even though I now suspect you're half-goblin,' he said, narrowing his eye.

'I knew it,' whispered Grace. 'It looks just like Cake Hunters! But with more bugs and fewer sprinkles . . .'

'Hurry up!' roared Ripper from further up the road.

'Actually, we're just going to pop in here and pick up some treats for when we get to your house,' called Grace. 'It's only polite!'

'Ha, you, polite!' laughed Mr Harris. 'As if.'

Grace ignored him as she pushed open the door and the bell jangled above them.

# CHAPTER THIRTY-THREE

# Blue Coat Lady

'Can I help?' said a familiar voice.

Grace froze.

A dark-haired woman stood behind the glass counter, her brown eyes twinkling. A long hat made her look taller than she was and her bright blue coat made Grace's world stand still for just a moment.

'There she is,' said Mr Harris. 'Blue coat lady. You're welcome.'

Grace fought the urge to kick the goblins out of the way and throw herself into her mum's arms.

'Mr Harris,' she whispered, 'that's my mum.

My *real* mum. I haven't seen her for a very long time. But we need to get away from these goblins, and then we need to leave Monster World. Please play along so we can get out safely.'

'I don't play along,' he retorted.

Grace glared at him. 'Please. You can have all the doughnuts you want, just please do this one thing.'

'ALL the doughnuts I want?' he said greedily. 'Fine. I'll play along.'

The goblins had rushed forward to order pickled pee bug pastries. When they had finished, Grace pushed forward and said quietly, 'Can I have a caramel bun, please?' Caramel buns were her favourite thing in the world.

Grace's mum's face became very still and she looked up slowly. As their eyes met, Grace stared hard, ignoring the tears that welled up in her eyes, and raised her finger to her lips, hoping her mum would understand what to do.

'Of course,' her mum said, dabbing at her eye with her long, trailing sleeve.

'And I'll have ALL the doughnuts,' said Mr Harris triumphantly.

'Not now,' hissed Grace.

'You said I could,' the cyclops spat back.

'Fine! And he will have all the doughnuts,' she muttered.

'No problem,' said Grace's mum. 'Do you think you could help me get one of the big boxes from out the back so I can fit them all in?'

'No! Do it yourself, it's your bakery,' snapped Mr Harris. He looked across at Grace, who scowled at him. 'Oh . . . I mean yes, yes, of course I'll help *you* get a box down in *your* bakery.'

'I'll come too,' said Grace.

Leaving the goblins behind them – Frank was now on the shoulders of the tallest one, Ripper – Grace and Mr Harris followed Grace's mum, Louisa, through the door behind the counter.

'Grace!'

'Mum!'

Grace threw herself into her mum's outstretched arms and hugged her so tightly she could barely breathe. A sob escaped her throat and she let the tears stream down her cheeks.

'For goodness' sake,' grumbled Mr Harris.

'How? How are you here?' said Louisa urgently.

'There's no time to explain, Mum, we have to go now!' said Grace. 'But this bakery, it looks just like Cake –'

181

'Hunters! Our bakery!' She nodded happily. 'Dad and I set this place up when we first arrived here.' She looked pointedly at Mr Harris.

He averted his eye and murmured something about lovely cakes.

She continued. 'Grace, do you know how we get back? Dad and I have looked and looked for a gateway but have found nothing! In two years!'

'You haven't looked properly. There's one right next door,' said Mr Harris, biting his nail. 'You're thick like her.' He pointed at Grace.

'Dad's here too! Where is he?' Grace asked, her eyes wide.

'Having a nap upstairs,' said Louisa. 'I'll go and get him now. He's going to be more than a little shocked.'

'Mum, can we get out of here through a back door?' asked Grace.

Louisa nodded.

Something knocked sharply on the door behind the counter. 'What are you doing back there? Frankenstein is hungry. Hurry up!'

'Frank! We have to get him back!' said Grace, looking at Mr Harris.

He shrugged. 'Just leave him. They seem to like him. And anyway, your dad's here – he can stay with him. Although I'm confused. How did he get here?'

'No! We can't leave him! And I need to explain about my dad. Mr Harris, the situation is not quite what I said . . .' Grace started.

'Doughnut Lady,' he growled. There was another thump on the door.

'Please!' pleaded Grace. 'We need to get poor Frank! NOW! I absolutely will not leave him here. Mum, can you get Dad, as quickly as possible?'

Louisa nodded and hurried away.

'Okay, I think what we need to do is –' Grace began.

'Shhh!' hissed Mr Harris. He thrust the door open, plucked Frank from Ripper's shoulders, then slammed the door shut again. In a flash, he shoved a chair under the handle and a shelving unit in front of the chair.

'There,' he said. 'No need for your fussing.'

'Oh, well done, Mr Harris!' said Grace in surprise.

'Thank you!' cried Frank, forgetting himself for a moment and flinging his arms around Mr Harris in a giant hug.

'Urgh! Get it off me,' whispered Mr Harris to Grace, holding his arms up in surrender.

'Frank,' blurted Grace. 'You've been so brave. If it wasn't for you, we would never have walked past this bakery! It's down to you that we've found my parents. Thank you so much!'

Frank smiled timidly, then flung his arms around her.

'GRACE!' a deep voice exclaimed.

Grace's brain took a moment to process what she saw. The gangly arms and legs, the scruffy hair, the slightly wonky glasses – and, most importantly, the enormous, beaming, joyful smile.

'Dad!' Grace ran towards him.

## CHAPTER THIRTY-FOUR

# Escape from Monster World

'Oh Grace, my darling girl,' her dad cried, his long arms squeezing her in a giant hug.

Thunderous knocking boomed from behind the shelving unit.

'Hang on! What do you mean, *Dad*?' asked Mr Harris, ignoring the muffled shouts of, 'Give me back my Franken-baby!' and, 'Ripper! Ripper them up NOW!'

He narrowed his eye. 'That's not your dad. Your dad has one arm and is annoying. Who are all these mums and dads? These goblins, sorceresses? This plain boring man?' he said pointing at Eamon.

'Mr Harris! There's no time to explain. The goblins are going to be through here any minute! To cut a long story short, this is my dad. My real dad. Max, the man I said was my dad, is actually Frank's dad, and that goblin just thinks she's his mum,' Grace gabbled.

'Our Max?' said her dad. 'And this is Frank! I've never met him. Hi Frank!'

The sound of smashing glass echoed down the corridor.

'We have to go!' cried Louisa. 'This way!'

They hurried forward but, in the commotion, Frank's fork clattered to the floor. He stopped to pick it up.

'This kid!' said Mr Harris in exasperation, striding back to Frank. 'Don't stop! Listen to the blue coat lady I ate once.' He picked Frank up and tucked him under his arm, exactly as he had done with Grace back at Hamleys.

They ran to a rickety wooden door at the end of the building. As they slammed it shut behind them, they heard the clatter of shelves falling to the ground.

'Quick!' shouted Eamon.

A troll sat in front of a wrought iron gate at the bottom of the garden.

'Oh, a back gate but . . . you've got to be joking,' said Mr Harris. 'I don't want to eat another troll. They taste disgusting!'

'Why on earth do you need to eat him?' asked Grace.

Mr Harris sighed heavily. 'You are so thick. I have to eat him because he's guarding the gate to Human World.'

'*That* is the gate to Human World?' yelled Eamon. 'In our garden?'

'The troll told me he keeps his billy goats through there!' exclaimed Louisa.

Mr Harris shook his head patronisingly. 'Then you are even thicker than Doughnut Lady. If that's possible.'

Footsteps rumbled through the bakery. Mr Harris strode to the troll, whose badge read *Ferdinand Spangles – Gate-Keeping Troll Trainee*, picked him up by his tuft of silver hair and dropped him into his mouth. He didn't chew, just swallowed the creature whole.

'Oh, the key!' he whined. 'Actually, doesn't matter.' He thrust Frank's arm forward, aiming the fork at the chunky padlock on the gate.

With a wiggle and a clunk, the lock sprang open.

'Terrible quality lock. Trolls are so cheap,' he said, disgusted. 'Come on then, thickos.' And he nudged the gate open with Frank's mass of curls.

# CHAPTER THIRTY-FIVE

# Neville

Grace, her mum and dad, and Mr Harris, who was still carrying Frank under his arm, stumbled through the gateway into a silent corridor. The stony, dusty path that had been under their feet was immediately replaced with a soft, plush carpet.

'Good grief!' exclaimed Eamon. 'This is the inside of 10 Downing Street! So we had a gateway at the bottom of our garden that led directly to Downing Street, for two years? I might actually cry.'

'But you're here now. Thanks to ME! Right, hero time. Even though I have literally *just* been one!' shouted Mr Harris.

'Hang on,' said Grace impatiently. 'Dad, do you know how to get to the Prime Minister's office?'

Eamon nodded. 'It's just down the next corridor.'

When they turned the corner, they saw Danni and Max. They were standing outside a door and Max was furiously typing numbers into a keypad. Every time he stopped, the keypad did an angry beep to tell him the sequence was wrong.

'Frank! Thanks heavens!' cried Max, easing him from the clamp of Mr Harris's arm.

'Mum? Dad!' Danni shrieked, throwing herself towards her parents, grabbing Grace on the way.

Mr Harris sighed loudly. 'Oh, happy to see them, are you, Lady I Don't Know? What about me? The hero?'

'Ignore him!' Grace said to Danni, who looked startled at the sight of the cyclops. She looked at Mr Harris. 'Right, are you actually going to be a hero, or not? That's the door we need to open.'

'Move please!' Mr Harris yelled, striding forward.

He took a deep breath, cracked his neck both ways, then his knuckles, and drew back his colossal arm. He thumped the door once. It gave a creak and immediately fell backwards into the Prime Minister's office.

The scene that greeted them inside the office was not a good one.

Neville, still looking startlingly like Max, was holding the Prime Minister in a headlock. His skin was going very slightly green and his arms were beginning to strain, as if they were trying to change shape. His eyes seemed to be taking on an unmistakable yellow tinge and they looked as though they were edging closer together.

Grace heard a rumbling growl from Mr Harris, who was next to her and pulling himself up to his full height. His chest was pushed out, his arms were tensed, and his legs were apart, as if he was getting ready to fight.

'Neville Adolphin Quentland Tommy Something Something Harris,' he spat venomously.

'Steve,' hissed Neville.

'*Steve?*' Grace blurted out, momentarily forgetting the overwhelming danger they were in. 'Your name is *Steve?*'

'Sssh!' said Mr Harris, not taking his eyes off his grandfather.

'But Steve what?' asked Grace. 'Surely you have middle names, like all cyclopes?'

'It's just Steve,' snapped Mr Harris. 'Ridiculous.'

'That's why you don't use it!' said Grace. 'You're embarrassed because it's not fancy enough!'

'DOUGHNUT LADY!' shouted Mr Harris. 'FOCUS!'

Neville threw his head back and laughed. A forked tongue darted between his lips.

'A disgraceful name for a disgraceful cyclops,' he said spitefully.

Mr Harris inched forward, his hands flexing, a threatening rumble emanating from his chest.

'And, heavens above, look at the size of you! A moment on the lips, forever on the hips,' Neville chided.

Mr Harris looked as if he might explode without the help of baking powder.

'What a shame I got here before you did.' Neville tightened his hold round the Prime Minister's neck.

Grace looked at Mrs Attwood. The poor woman was as white as a sheet, her hands locked on to Neville's arm at her throat.

Mr Harris let out a guttural roar so forceful, Grace felt her hair lift from her shoulders. He lurched across the room. Before he had even got to Neville, he was forced backwards so hard, he hit the wall at the back of the office.

Neville laughed. 'Pathetic! I thought you might present a bit of a challenge, but it seems I was wrong. You're just like the rest of these useless creatures. So now you can all watch me finish off Prime Minister Battwood.'

'It's Prime Minister *Attwood*,' spat Mr Harris, launching himself forward unexpectedly. This time, he took Neville by surprise. He shot across the room and raised one huge arm at lightning speed, ready to strike his grandfather with all his

might. But he wasn't fast enough. Neville grabbed him by the throat with his free hand and lifted Mr Harris off the ground easily.

'Get off him!' screamed Grace.

Neville's gaze locked on to her. His eyes had merged into one large, bright yellow one in the middle of his forehead. Its black pupil was oval, giving him a distinctly reptilian look which Grace was not at all keen on.

'Get off him?' he mimicked. 'Is he your friend, little Hunter girl?' He spat 'Hunter'.

'Yes, actually, he sort of is,' said Grace, feeling suddenly rather fond of Mr Harris.

Neville threw back his head and laughed. 'How embarrassing, Steve! So you're not just hideously large, you're also a soft touch! A coward. You are an embarrassment to our kind, you human-loving urchin.'

Neville growled the last few words. The sound of his venomous voice made the tiny hairs on the back of Grace's neck stand on end. Mr Harris struggled, legs flailing, his hand gripping his grandfather's forearm.

'Put me down and fight!' he wheezed.

'No, I won't be doing that,' said Neville casually.

'Yes, you will!' yelled Grace, shrugging off her rucksack and running towards him.

## CHAPTER THIRTY-SIX

# Mr Harris Helps

With both hands busy, there wasn't a lot Neville could do to stop Grace punching his snake-like eye with all the force she could muster. He howled and instinctively drew his hands up to his face, letting go of the Prime Minister and Mr Harris in the process.

'Mr Harris!' screeched Grace. 'Protect her!' She waved an arm towards the Prime Minister, who was trying to scramble away. Mr Harris reacted instantly. He grabbed Mrs Attwood with one meaty hand and shoved her behind him, moving backwards.

Grace frantically reached towards the pocket which had contained her precious pot of baking powder.

'No, no, no!' she whispered, finding the zip undone and the pocket empty. Before she could make a run for it, a scaly hand, which had grown black shiny talons in place of fingernails, darted out and grabbed her by the hair.

'Grace!' yelled Eamon, running towards her.

Neville shot out his free hand and, in a flash, slammed Eammon against the far wall of the office. Grace watched in horror as her dad struggled to get up, seemingly bound by invisible ties. Her mum stood protectively in front of Danni, and Max held Frank behind him. Their eyes were the only things giving away their panic.

Slowly, Grace found herself being pulled backwards, hair first, until she could feel – and, unfortunately, smell – Neville's breath, by the side of her face. It was worse than Mr Harris's, which really was saying something.

'What did you do?' he snarled.

'I punched you in your massive, ugly eye,' said Grace, having decided if she was about to die, then she might as well go down in a blaze of glory.

Neville pulled her hair hard. 'Why would you disrespect something as powerful as me?'

'Because you don't deserve respect,' Grace replied. 'And I will *not* stand by and watch you try to take over our world.'

'You won't need to, little girl, you'll be long gone!' Neville bellowed. He had barely any resemblance to Max any more. His black, greasy hair was slicked back from his snake-like eye and he opened his mouth impossibly wide, revealing his skinny, forked tongue and hundreds of razor-sharp teeth.

'Doughnut Lady!'

Grace's eyes darted towards Mr Harris, who stood at the other end of the

room, his arm poised in a throw position. With Neville holding her by the hair, Grace's hands were free to catch the pot that hurtled towards her like a bullet. The moment she caught it, she flipped off the lid, twisted round and hurled the contents into Neville's eye. For good measure, she chucked the pot into his mouth.

For a moment, nothing happened.

She felt Neville shake with anger as he let out a roar more forceful than the sound a pride of lions could produce. Grace shut her eyes tightly and braced herself for what was coming. There was nothing more she could do. She had tried her hardest. And they had managed to save her parents – which was the most important thing of all.

A voice interrupted her thoughts. 'Grace! Move!'

Suddenly, she was swept backwards by her dad, who had escaped his invisible bonds and rushed

over to her. He half-carried her to the back of the room, where her mum, Danni, Max, Frank, Mr Harris and the Prime Minister stood, staring in the direction she had come from.

She turned.

Neville was dragging himself along the carpet towards them. The shape of his limbs was constantly changing: from man-sized, to super-human-sized, to very small indeed. His head morphed from cyclops, to snake, to Bertram, to Max, to a hideously ugly, scaly mess. And all the time he got closer . . . and closer.

'What do we do?' wailed Mrs Attwood.

'We hope, with everything we've got, Prime Minister,' whispered Max, his eyes not moving from Neville.

Grace frantically patted her pockets, looking for anything she could use against him. The contents of her rucksack had spilled across the floor when she dropped her bag, and there were crumbs, pencils, broken bits of biscuits and scraps of paper everywhere. She lunged towards a squashed yellow paper bag from the bakery, which was the nearest thing to her.

'Please be the special ones,' she whispered.

The bag had ripped, revealing mushy-looking rings of dough.

'Doughnuts!' exclaimed Mr Harris delightedly. He seemed to have momentarily forgotten all about Neville. Then, realising what she was about to do, he cried, 'NO! Don't waste them on him!'

Grace hurled the paper bag at Neville, who was now only a few metres away. As it flew through the air, doughnuts hurtled in every direction. Several bounced off his muscular arms, but one went straight into his snake-like eye.

'YOU!' His voice made the floor rumble and he crawled towards Grace.

Out of nowhere, Frank appeared, his fork poised

in one hand. The other hand pulled back an elastic band, caught on the prongs, and a sharp-looking shard of ginger nut biscuit. With a war-like cry, Frank's skinny arms catapulted the biscuit towards Neville. It hit him square in the eye, point first.

Neville stopped dead. He began to glow and tremor.

'Cover your eyes!' yelled Max.

Grace threw her hands up just as a deafening whistling filled the room. She braced herself for an almighty bang, putting her hands over her ears and bending her head forward, chin against her chest, eyes squeezed shut.

But the bang didn't come. Instead, there was a breathy *poof* . . . then nothing.

Cautiously, Grace opened one eye, hoping she wouldn't find a fully re-formed Neville looming in front of her.

She didn't. The room was empty and still. The only sign that Neville had ever been there was a scorch mark on the carpet and a tiny, torn-off scrap of yellow paper bag.

CHAPTER THIRTY-SEVEN

# A Gift for a Cyclops

Mrs Attwood slumped into the big leather chair behind the shiny wooden desk, one hand on her chest, the other flopped over the arm-rest.

'Are you feeling all right, Prime Minister?' asked Max.

'Yes, I think so,' she replied, straightening up. 'I'm used to dealing with a lot of situations, but not generally those in which I might be attacked by a murderous cyclops called Neville.'

'You were very brave,' said Eamon, his arms around Grace protectively. 'It must have been a terrifying experience.'

The Prime Minister nodded and stood up, smoothing down her skirt. 'That's one way of putting it,' she said. 'Anyway, enough about me. I believe thanks are in order. Thank you, young lady, from the very bottom of my heart. You are extraordinarily brave. As are you, young man.'

She held out her hand to Grace, then to Frank. He transferred his fork to the other hand

in order to shake her hand properly. Grace saw how proud he looked and felt an overwhelming surge of fondness for him.

'Heavens above, you saved my life!' the Prime Minister said, pulling Grace and Frank towards her and enveloping them in a hug.

There was a loud cough from the corner of the room, where Mr Harris stood.

Mrs Attwood turned. 'I was coming to you next, Mr Harris,' she said. 'Thank you too, very much.'

'Are you going to shake my hand?' asked Mr Harris.

'Will you eat me if I do?' asked Mrs Attwood politely.

Mr Harris shook his head. 'Only if you don't.'

Grace shot him a look.

The Prime Minister offered her hand to the cyclops.

Mr Harris, with lightning speed, darted forward, grabbed it and gave it a long, wet lick.

'No!' Grace leapt towards him but Mr Harris shot out his other meaty hand and stopped her in her tracks.

'Don't panic, Doughnut Lady!' he grumbled. 'I was just checking what she would have tasted like. And now I don't want to eat her anyway. I was expecting peanut butter and I got . . . celery. Yuck. Bitter. Not a fan at all.'

'Mr Harris! Apologise!' cried Grace.

'Have a sense of humour,' retorted the cyclops. 'I am heroic AND fun.'

The Prime Minister offered her hand to him again, averting her eyes from the sheen of saliva he had deposited on it. Max and Eamon moved closer. Mr Harris shook it properly and tutted loudly.

'What's the matter?' asked Mrs Attwood.

'Doughnut Lady, who's quite mean, told me that I can't eat you *and* I can't be Prime Minister. I only actually wanted to speak to you about a couple of very important matters. I probably wouldn't have eaten you. And I definitely won't, now I know you taste of celery,' said Mr Harris petulantly. 'Everything is *very* disappointing, especially because I have been such a BIG help.'

'Well, I'm not ready to give up my position as Prime Minister of the United Kingdom, I'm afraid, Mr Harris. But I am happy to find the time to speak about your important issues, if that helps?' said Mrs Attwood. 'I must also say how glad I am you have taken Grace's advice not to eat me, celery-flavoured or otherwise. Although I am rather surprised.' She stepped back a couple of paces.

Mr Harris sighed loudly. 'I *had* to. She sort of helped a bit, just then, when *I* destroyed Neville Aldolphick Something Else Stupid Long Name Harris. And, annoyingly, I *promised* that I wouldn't eat you. If I make a promise, I don't break it. Which, thinking about it, is ridiculous. I thought it was noble, but it's actually just stupid. No offence, but

I would definitely be a better Prime Minister than you are. Can I sit in your chair?'

Mrs Attwood nodded and gestured towards the chair.

Mr Harris shot past her at lightning speed and plopped his massive form into the leather, which creaked under his weight. He swung his feet up onto the desk.

'Mr Harris, before I go, please do give me an overview of what you would like to discuss with me.' said the Prime Minister.

Mr Harris nodded importantly. 'Very well.' He sat up straight. 'Issue number one. Rights for monsters. We have none. Which is unacceptable. Some monsters are actually quite pleasant and live here in Human World, keeping themselves to themselves. They should have rights.'

'Okay,' said the Prime Minister, looking rather surprised. 'That sounds reasonable.'

Mr Harris held up two beefy fingers. 'Issue number two. Bicycle facilities in London are appalling. Monsters love riding bicycles so it's high time someone arranged some good quality bikes to hire and decent storage facilities for those who have purchased their own. The bikes at the docking stations are rubbish. The quality is terrible. Come to think of it, did a troll choose them?'

Mrs Attwood shrugged. 'Not that I'm aware of. Anyway, Mr Harris, I'm sure we can find a solution to both those issues. Now, is there a number three?' she ventured.

'Not for the moment,' Mr Harris said curtly.

'Very well. Let me think about some proposals to address your issues. Max, could you arrange a more formal meeting that starts less dangerously?' She turned back to the cyclops. 'Now, one last thing, Mr Harris. In the information I have seen about you, there was a mention of your interest in the board game Snakes and Ladders. Is that right?'

The cyclops looked up. 'Yes. I'm unbeatable. Do you play?'

'Sometimes, with my grandchildren,' she replied, reaching into a highly polished cabinet and pulling out an old, intricately carved wooden box. 'I'd like you to have this. As a token of my thanks.' She held it out to him. 'It's one of the oldest versions of Snakes and Ladders you'll ever find. It was a gift from the President of India, where the game originated. Perhaps it was fate that he gave it to me all those years ago.'

Mr Harris took the box and opened it, running his sausage-like fingers along the carvings and sniffing it loudly.

'Did you know, Mr Harris,' said Mrs Attwood, 'that in the original version of the game, the ladders represented virtues? They showed that anyone could claim salvation through doing good. I think you did that today.'

'I did!' said Mr Harris, clutching the box to his chest. 'I'm virtuous!'

'I'm sorry you can't be Prime Minister,' Mrs Attwood said, 'but, as I said, I'm not ready to give up my job, and thankfully, you have promised not to eat me . . . '

'Yet,' he muttered.

'Ever!' cried Grace.

'Fine, ever. Whatever,' Mr Harris mumbled.

'Anyway,' the Prime Minister continued, 'given that you've shown remarkable restraint, I'd like to take a rather unusual step. I would like to offer you a job.'

## CHAPTER THIRTY-EIGHT

# Mr Harris Gets a Job

Mrs Attwood straightened her shoulders and continued. 'It's an important job working with our Secret Service, to identify monsters living among us.'

'That does sound important,' said Mr Harris, swinging his feet off the desk. 'And monsters having jobs is one of the monster rights I want to discuss with you.'

'Well, there you are,' the Prime Minister replied, smiling. 'I hope you will take me up on my offer, but you must understand there will be conditions, such as not eating people, which we can discuss another time. Perhaps over the phone, thinking about it, rather than in person.'

'Hmm.' Mr Harris frowned. 'Very well. So, what *can* I eat?'

'Virtually anything *except* humans, I would imagine,' Louisa offered helpfully. 'Don't worry about that now, Mr Harris. Will you take the job?'

'I'll have to think about it,' he said pompously. 'I'm very busy. Perhaps I'll do it part-time, or as a job share.'

Grace rolled her eyes.

'Of course,' agreed Mrs Attwood. 'Max, will you please let me know what decision Mr Harris makes?'

Max nodded.

'Very well.' The Prime Minister addressed everyone in the room. 'Thank you all, once again. I'm indebted to each of you.'

As they left 10 Downing Street, Mr Harris pushed past them, his wooden box clamped firmly under his arm.

'Mr Harris!' shouted Grace. 'Where are you going?'

He turned. 'Not that it's any of your business, Doughnut Lady, but I intend to visit my cousin, Carmelita-Florentina Davina Matilda the third.' Danni sniggered behind Grace.

'Oh right. Well, have a nice time,' said Grace. 'And thanks for not eating Mrs Attwood.'

Mr Harris waved his arm in the air dismissively as he strode forward. 'Yes, whatever, bye, Doughnut Lady, and Doughnut Lady's mum and dad, and man who I thought was Mr Doughnut Lady', his puny child, and the girl I don't know . . .' He carried on muttering as he disappeared swiftly down the road.

'Should we just let him go like that?' asked Louisa. 'What if he eats someone?'

'Don't worry, darling,' said Eamon. 'Half of

the Secret Service will be on his tail.'

Louisa nodded, her arms around her girls'
shoulders, her peacock-blue coat, minus the
feather, soft against Grace's face.

Max was standing with his hand on Frank's
shoulder. Although his fork was still in his hand,
it was by his side and Frank was smiling.

'Thanks again, Frank. I'm not sure we'd be here without you,' said Grace, grinning.

'Hear, hear!' shouted Eamon.

'You're welcome,' Frank replied. 'I'm working on being as brave as you one day.'

'You already are,' said Grace.

CHAPTER THIRTY-NINE

# Dinner Time!

As the Hunter family walked away, Mr Harris held up his hand to stop a black cab.

'Where to, mate?' asked the taxi driver.

'The London Palladium,' said Mr Harris.

'Gotcha. That's where they're filming *Britain's Got Talent*, ain't it?'

Mr Harris giggled silently behind his massive hand. 'Yes,' he replied demurely.

'You gonna watch?' asked the driver.

'Watch?' said Mr Harris. 'No! I'm doing something much more important than that.'

'You auditioning? What's your act? Is it juggling?

You look like you could be a juggler with them big hands,' said the driver cheerily.

'I don't juggle. Juggling is stupid,' snapped Mr Harris, then his face broke into a grotesque smile. 'I'm a magician!'

The driver nodded encouragingly in his rear-view mirror. 'Everyone loves a magician. What sort of magic? Card tricks? Stuff with coins?'

'It's a disappearing act,' Mr Harris said, sniggering. 'I make people disappear.'

'Clever!' said the driver enthusiastically. 'I'll get you there as fast as I can in this traffic, mate.'

'Yes. I must be quick,' said Mr Harris, leaning back into the leather seat and rubbing his giant hands together. His bulging stomach gurgled. 'I'm having a bite to eat first . . . and I've invited the head judge to join me.'

**The End**
(nearly)

**Name**: Mr Harris

**Type**: Cyclops

**Age**: Approximately 352

**Height**: 2.05 metres

**Weight**: 285 lbs

**Strengths**: 14 detected: power, sense of smell, body mass, confidence, keeping promises, Snakes and Ladders, fighting skills, eyesight, ability to hypnotise, memory, regeneration, Frisbee, chess, passion for monster rights.

**Weaknesses**: 1 detected: iced doughnuts.

**Likes**: Iced doughnuts, being important, politics, eating people who annoy him, board games, jokes, bicycles, *Britain's Got Talent*.

**Dislikes**: Rude humans, too many humans, avocados, his grandfather, Neville Harris.

**Best form of destruction**: Iced doughnuts, baking powder, sharp object to centre of eye.

**Notes**: Tendency to eat people with little or no warning, although some improvement recently.

Friendship: 3 (+3)

Size: 93 (+6)

Courage: 85 (+11)

Kindness: 1 (+1)

Intelligence: 71 (please note, above average for this breed of monster)

Loyalty: 1 (+1)

Violence: 99

Danger: 99 (-1)

What will Grace and Mr Harris get up to next?

Read on for a sneak peek at the next book

in the series . . .

# CHAPTER ONE

# Grace vs Bath Dweller

Grace yanked the tentacle out of her nose, turning her head to wipe the trail of snot-like slime off her face, as she held the squirming monster at arm's length over the bath. The master bathroom in the House by the River was usually gleaming white and peaceful. Today, not so much.

'Mr Harris!' she yelled. 'For goodness sake! HELP!'

The cyclops lowered the TV magazine he was holding and peered over the top.

'What's the matter?' he replied impatiently. 'I'm trying to read.'

Grace slapped another tentacle away from her ear with her free hand and turned her head just in time to avoid a squirt of foul-smelling liquid.

'What do you think is the matter? Look! You're meant to be learning how to do this! We're on a training exercise!' she cried. 'This Bath Dweller is crazy. It has more tentacles than I've ever seen and I'm struggling to get it under control! You're just sitting there reading, when you should be helping!'

Mr Harris raised the magazine back in front of his face and muttered from behind it, 'I am learning. I know that Bath Dwellers are not dangerous. The worst they can do is stick their tentacles to you and squirt you with grotty water. So stop making a fuss.'

Grace shook her head, like a wet dog, in an attempt to get at least four tentacles out of her long dark hair. 'You say they're not dangerous but what if it puts its tentacles over my nose and mouth? What would happen then?'

Mr Harris lowered the magazine again. 'Oh, well then you would die.'

'Then, HELP ME! I've got no hands left to get the lemon meringue pie!' shouted Grace, suddenly clamping her mouth shut as another tentacle prodded her lip.

The cyclops snapped the magazine shut. 'That's bad training, you should never put yourself in that position. And you've ruined my ME time. You're so dramatic, Doughnut Lady! Oh, it could kill me. Oh, it has so many tentacles. Oh, where's my exploding cakes? Oh, help me, amazing Mr Harris, help me . . .' He tutted and shook his enormous head.

If one of Grace's hands had been free, she would definitely have slapped him. Despite his vastness, and his tendency to eat people and other monsters, with very little warning, she wasn't remotely scared of him. She was a twelfth-generation monster hunter after all. And, since they had been thrust together in an unlikely friendship having saved the Prime Minister's life just the week before, she was oddly fond of the obnoxious creature.

Grace closed her eyes as the Bath Dweller's tentacles suckered almost every part of her face in an effort to make her release her grip, so she didn't see Mr Harris heave himself off the closed toilet lid and shuffle over.

Suddenly, Grace felt all the pressure from the suckers disappear, some even made popping sounds as they lifted from her skin. She opened her eyes to see Mr Harris looming in front of her.

'Gone. I don't know what all the fuss was about,' said Mr Harris, licking the end of his massive finger.

'Did you eat it?' Grace asked.

Mr Harris belched. 'Yuck. Tasted like tuna that's gone off. I wouldn't recommend that you sample one.'

'Why would you eat it? They stink!' Grace said in disbelief.

'What else did you want me to do with it?' Mr Harris snapped. 'Put a bonnet on it and pop it on my shoulder? You were all screechy and it was the quickest way to get rid of it. And, anyway, I was hungry. Not a word of thanks, as usual.'

'You're always hungry,' said Grace, rolling her eyes. 'And, thank you.'

Mr Harris frowned but then sniggered.

'What?' asked Grace. 'What's funny?'

'Your face is funny,' he giggled. 'You have spots all over it where it stuck its suckers to you. You look DISGUSTING. But funny.'

'Great,' said Grace flatly. 'Glad I amuse you. You do realise you can't do this when you officially start working for the Secret Service next week?'

'Do what?' the cyclops asked irritably.

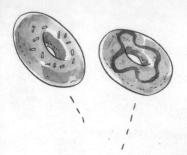

'Have me time while you're out on a monster hunting mission. You'll either have to get the job done on your own, or you'll have to work as part of a team. Either way, you'll have to put in a lot of effort all the time,' said Grace.

'I am too important to work as part of a team,' the cyclops said smugly. 'I destroyed my evil grandfather and, in doing so, saved the Prime Minister's life. All in the space of a few minutes. I am a hero, Doughnut Lady, I will probably just have to sit in my great big office and sign things.'

'WE destroyed Neville and WE saved the Prime Minister's life. Seriously, you start on Monday, have you not read your job description yet? You're a part-time Field Officer working for the Secret Service. That means you'll have to go out and do actual missions – although why you're only part time, I have no idea,' Grace said, shaking her head in bewilderment. 'You were offered the job because of your monster knowledge – you know, what with you being one yourself. You'll never just be in an office!'

'You don't know anything,' said Mr Harris.

'I know that you'll be on the front-line,' Grace retorted. 'It'll be hard work and it'll be dangerous. You really need to read the information, Mr Harris.'

'You can help me with the hard work and the danger,' he replied flatly.

'No, I can't,' said Grace. 'I'm only working with you over the summer holidays to show you what to do. Then I'll be back at school and you'll have to carry on without me.'

'Fine. You're annoying. I'll be glad of the break,' the cyclops mumbled.

'Well, you've got five more weeks of me yet!' said Grace, cheerfully. 'Right, let's go downstairs and find Frank. He'll be pleased the Bath Dweller has gone.'

# MONSTER GLOSSARY

### Bath Dweller

Related to Slime Imps, Bath Dwellers are a similar jelly-like texture but have a multitude of tentacles. Invisible to humans over the age of ten, they are often the reason children scream their heads off at the mere mention of a nice soak in the bath.

### Button Gobbler

Lost another button? BGs will pick them directly off your coat, or your school shirt, with their razor-sharp teeth. Don't bother looking for the ones that disappear either, they will have been digested within seconds.

## Cyclops

One-eyed and usually very large, cyclopes made regular appearances in Greek and Roman mythology. Since then, they've evolved in a fascinating way. While most are still as thick as custard, some have gained intelligence. Most are self-important, some are power-crazed, many are happy to eat the problems they are presented with, especially if those problems are humans or gate-keeping trolls, and ALL of them love board games.

## Giant

Super-sized person, looks human but eats whole cows. This species is, ironically, often fond of very small things, for example, thimbles, dolls' houses and mice.

## Goblin

If you Google a goblin, you'll be told they are mythical creatures who are almost always small and mischievous (or outright malicious) and greedy, especially for gold and jewels. This is partially true. What Google doesn't tell you is that they come in many forms and breeds, including; large-eared, small-eared, pointy-eared, lesser-wrinkled and sharp-toothed. They are generally stupid and unpleasant and will often resort to violence, even when a sensible chat could sort out a tricky situation.

## Gorgon

The less said about these hissy horrors the better. They have hair made of snakes and they'll turn you to stone as soon as they'll look at you. Interestingly, they are great lovers of cheese and most forms of crackers. Nuff said.

## Hair Knotter (sidekick - Hairband Thief)

Anyone who has long hair will understand the agony of brushing it first thing in the morning. How does it get so knotty? You've been asleep, lying still, for goodness' sake! The answer is Hair Knotters. These tangly teasers are always happy to hop onto your head and quite literally tie your hair into knots. They are often found paired with their sidekick, a Hairband Thief. Guess what Hairband Thieves do when your hair is finally knot-free and you've stopped begging your mum to leave you alone? They flick your hairbands as far away as possible with their freakishly strong index finger and thumb (the rest of their digits are tiny and weak). That's why you always find the lost bands somewhere bizarre, like behind the sofa.

## Homework Taker

The clue is in the name of these sneaky creatures. Their favourite thing in the world is that homework you painstakingly put in your school bag ready to hand in. They will swipe it and read it, and you'll most likely never see it again. Unless it's boring. Then they will put it back somewhere you thought you had looked for it.

## Loaf Licker

You know when the bread goes mouldy and everyone is cross because they really wanted a piece of toast? It's because a Loaf Licker has licked the bread. LLs mainly lick the crusts but never actually bite into them. And their breath is SO awful, it turns the bread green and furry.

## Mess Maker

Why is it that your bedroom often looks much messier than it was when you went downstairs for dinner? Look no further than the Mess Maker monster who enjoys nothing more than un-tidying your room. These scruffy looking, colourful hairballs will shred tissues, play catch with the contents of your drawers and rearrange your toys in the blink of an eye. Sociable and real team players, they often work in groups.

## Mutant Vampire Bat

The clue is in the title. These are vampire bats where something has gone badly wrong. Sometimes it's their hairstyle, sometimes it's the size of their wings. Other times it's the fact that they will sink their mutant fangs into your neck quicker than you can say, 'do you know Dracula?'

## Parent Punisher

Now, these are interesting monsters. They don't take kindly to children being told off so when this sort of unpleasant scenario occurs, they will almost always do something to take revenge against the teller-offer. Whether it's a tiny poo in their coffee granules, or a quick wipe of their toothbrush round the toilet, these creatures are known for their loyalty to kids everywhere, and their wild creativity in punishments.

## Pie Pincher

Pie Pinchers lurk around bakeries and the pastry section in supermarkets. There is no pie this funny little beast won't pinch. Apple, cherry, pecan, chicken and ham, steak and ale, butternut squash and asparagus – anything with a pastry lid is at risk.

## Poo Shuffler

Have you ever trodden in a dog poo you just didn't see? You probably only found out because you trod it into the carpet when you got home and your dad went nuts. Poo Shufflers do exactly what their name suggests. They shuffle poos into your path, watch the consequences and laugh. A lot.

Poo Shuffler - -

## Shadow Stalker

Ever had that funny feeling something's watching you pick your nose, or lurking in the shadows of your brother's stinky bedroom, or chasing you up the stairs – even though there's nothing there?

Well, mostly, there isn't, so get a grip . . . ! But sometimes, in extreme cases, it's a Shadow Stalker. Don't worry, they can't hurt anyone and they can only exist where there are shadows, but they can make their presence felt, and that's enough for most of us to be turning every light on in the house immediately FOREVER.

## Slime Imp

Jelly like, and territorial within their chosen sewers, Slime Imps often appear through sink plugholes and scare children. They are drawn to the smell of mint, which is unfortunate, given where most of us clean our teeth.

## Snack Snaffler

These large-handed creatures will eat anything. Crisps, biscuits, sweets, they're not fussy (although they're not keen on rice cakes – too bland). If you're snacking on it, they will try and steal it. Or they'll lurk under your seat in the hope you'll drop something. They're hugely helpful in larger venues, such as concert halls and schools though.

## Snot-nosed Ogre

These Snot-nosed Ogres are large and not very clever. As their name would suggest, they have constantly runny noses, which makes them very angry creatures. They are known to enjoy a good punch-up and they like eating the odd human or large mammal. Luckily, they can be distracted quite easily with shiny objects, kaleidoscopes or ice cream. If you happen to have all three of those things with you, you'll probably make a snotty friend for life.

## Sock Stealer

These monsters are responsible for missing/odd socks and are always found wearing the ones they've taken on their legs. They often live inside tumble driers as the pickings are rich. They are surprisingly hostile for a creature with a liking for hosiery.

Sock Stealer --

GIVE ME SOCKS!

## Sorceress

A woman of magic. Like a wizard but with bags of girl power.

## Tripper Upper

You know when you trip over absolutely nothing, and your mum says you're clumsy? Well, it's not always you being clumsy, it's often a Tripper Upper being mischievous. These monsters camouflage into whichever floor they are lurking on and think it's hilarious when they pop up and trip you over.

## Troll

If you look up trolls, you'll likely find out that they are said to be creatures who dwell in isolated rocks, mountains, or caves, live together in small family units, and are rarely helpful to human beings. All true. They are also usually grumpy and impressed by silly things like power and fame. Believe it or not, most trolls like having jobs (they think it makes them important). Most enjoy careers in security and administration, or more specifically as traffic wardens and doctors'
receptionists. Additional,
random fact – they
LOVE cutlery.

Troll - -

## Under the Bed Beast (UTBB)

These wispy creatures live under children's beds. While they are generally small and weak, they are quite often to blame for children being scared at night and unable to get to sleep. Not dangerous though. Phew.

## Vegetable Nibbler

If you know someone who grows vegetables in their garden, you may well have heard them shout, 'What is eating my cabbages?!'. They will blame rabbits, slugs, snails, birds and sometimes even their neighbours. They're wrong. Vegetable Nibblers are almost always responsible.

## Wardrobe Lurker

WLs reside in children's wardrobes and often startle the children in question when they have failed to properly hide. They're often the cause of small children believing something scary lives in their wardrobe. The fact they are nocturnal doesn't help.

## Werewolf

You probably already know what a werewolf is but I bet there's a few things you don't know! For example, were you aware that most werewolves love singing, particularly karaoke, and have a flair for cooking? They can whip up a delicious sauce quicker than Jamie Oliver. They're also a bit short-tempered and bitey but, there you are, none of us are perfect.

## Yeti

In folklore, these are ape-like creatures, larger than humans, and said to inhabit the Himalayan Mountains. They are, in fact, highly sophisticated creatures who often choose a life of solitude, dedicated to the arts or academia. They hate arguing or conflict which is why they mostly choose to live in the mountains, where other, shoutier monsters can't bother them.

# MONSTER PROFILE

**Name:** Gianna Pollero

**Type:** Author

**Age:** 42 years

**Height:** 5'2"

**Weight:** Not telling you.

**Strengths:** 4 detectable: kindness, sense of adventure, writing skills (hopefully) and sense of humour.

**Weaknesses:** 3 detectable: jelly sweets, cute animals, home décor shops.

**Likes:** Reading, writing, chocolate, animals, gardening, photography, arty things, coffee, Italy, interior design, architecture and fruit jellies.

**Dislikes:** Rudeness, artichokes, anyone unkind, being cold and wasps.

**Best form of destruction:** One tonne of jelly sweets. I will eat them and explode.

**NOTES:** This monster likes to curl up with a cup of coffee and a book on a regular basis. When disturbed, she's very grumpy.

**SCORING:**
Friendship: 100
Size: 40
Courage: 62
Kindness: 93
Intelligence: 76
Loyalty: 90
Violence: 0
Danger: 5

**Type:** MEDIUM RARE

# MONSTER PROFILE

**Name:** Sarah Horne

**Type:** Illustrator

**Age:** Unknown. Experts guess between 0-862 years old.

**Height:** 5' 6"

**Weight:** Somewhere between a flea and a sumo wrestler.

**Strengths:** Can draw pretty much anything, Joy, Compassion, Fun.

**Weaknesses:** Stationery, Tuc biscuits or any manner of biscuit.

**Likes:** Drawing silly things, running up hills, Fruit and Nut Chocolate, music and a good poo joke.

**Dislikes:** A lie, impatient drivers and seaweed.

**Best form of destruction:** Too much chit-chatting about nothing at all.

**Notes:** A Sarah is an elusive creature. In the wild she can be found painting large canvases. Sarahs are especially drawn to joy and whimsy, stories (especially the silly ones) and she loves creative, big-picture people.

**SCORING:**

**Friendship:** 100

**Size:** 55

**Courage:** 71

**Kindness:** 90

**Intelligence:** 72

**Loyalty:** 06

**Violence:** 0

**Danger:** 0.000000001

# Acknowledgements

The biggest thank you imaginable goes to my daughter, Sophia. Without her, this book would never have been written and I owe the very foundations of Mr Harris, as a character, to her entirely. She has played a huge part in making my writing dreams come true and no words will ever be enough.

Massive thanks also to my son, Oscar. He's amazing and has unfailingly read and critiqued approximately six hundred versions of this book. He's always supportive and encouraging, and has no idea how much he has helped me through the writing process.

I'm the luckiest mum in the world.

Huge thanks go to my amazing family and friends who I am so lucky to have – my wonderful mum Lesley, my right arm Maria, Tracey, Helen,

Lindsay, Gemma, Annmarie, Jo, Carly (and in fact all the wonderful Johnsons), Aarti, Hannah and Richard, who have supported me, read my words, listened to my moans and encouraged me all the way.

Thanks also to Ant for many years of belief that it would happen.

And to the Curtis Brown Creative Class of 2016 – I just wouldn't be here without you and all your invaluable help and honesty. Gillian and Clare, thank you a million times over, for everything.

Gratitude to work friends and colleagues, past and present, especially Ruth and Lynne, who have listened and motivated, and to those who have bought me enormous celebratory chocolate cakes (you know who you are but you've had a mention already!). To Darren, Claire, Laura and all my old MTW buddies, thank you too.

An ear-splitting cheer please, everybody, for my spectacular agent, Rachel Mann, and everyone else at the Jo Unwin Literary Agency, who are quite simply some of the nicest people you could ever wish to meet. You've changed my life and I am beyond grateful.

And another one, just as loud, for all at Piccadilly Press (Bonnier), and my completely wonderful editor, Georgia Murray, who could see where this book needed to go from the very beginning and helped me make it the best it could be. I knew from the moment I walked in to my first meeting at Bonnier, that it was the perfect home for Grace, Mr Harris and all our other fabulous characters and monsters. I'll never forget the unbelievably thoughtful and creative lengths everyone went to, which made me feel like I had written something worth reading.

Last, but by no means least, thank you to all those who have bought my book and enjoyed it enough to read these acknowledgements

You'll never know how much it means.